The Heartbreaker

MADDIE JAMES

SAND DUNE BOOKS

The Heartbreaker

Maddie James

A Falls Mountain Romance, Book 3

About Falls Mountains

Welcome to Harbor Falls—where second chances bloom, hearts heal, and love finds its way home in the Blue Ridge Mountains.

The *Falls Mountain Romance* series delivers heartfelt, semi-sweet love stories filled with small-town charm, found family, and the promise of new beginnings. Each book can be read as a standalone story, but together they celebrate the beauty of hope, healing, and happily ever after.

But on Falls Mountain, love has a habit of showing up unannounced.

From second chances to secret babies to grumpy-sunshine pairings, each book brings a satisfying happily-ever-after and a cast of characters you'll want to visit again and again.

Falls Mountain Romance is a companion series to the Sweet Hart Inn Romance books by Maddie James.

The Heartbreaker

A Falls Mountain Romance, Book 3

Can a small-town doctor heal the one heart he broke long ago?

Dr. Sam Kirk was Lucki Stevenson's childhood best friend... and her teenage heartbreak. Now he's back in Harbor Falls, charmingly handsome, and living next door. Worse? He's more irresistible than she remembers.

But Lucki learned her lesson years ago: Sam Kirk is trouble for her heart.

She won't fall for the boy next door again. Not even if he's all grown up and determined to win her back.

Lucki has enough on her plate—coaching moody teenagers, dodging an annoying coworker, and trying to ignore the town busybodies who notice everything. So when Sam starts showing signs that he wants more than friendship, she braces herself for disaster. After all, he broke her heart once. She won't give him the chance to do it twice.

But Sam is a man who knows what he wants.

And what he wants—what he's always wanted—is Lucki.

This time, he's not giving up—not on her, not on them, and not on the future he should have fought for years ago. Between church shenanigans, chocolate milkshakes, BB-gun mishaps, and the interference of half the town, Sam launches a full-scale campaign to win Lucki's heart once and for all.

But can he prove he's not the heartbreaker she remembers?

A laugh out loud, slow-burn, second-chance romance about best friends turned lovers, small-town chaos, and embracing the love that was always meant to be.

Why You'll Love It

- Heartfelt **best-friends-to-lovers** and **second-chance romance**
- A swoony **boy-next-door doctor** who finally knows what he wants
- A heroine who protects her heart fiercely...and loves even fiercer
- Laugh out loud humor and small-town moments (and plenty of meddling!)
- Emotional depth + cozy warmth = satisfying happily-ever-after

Chapter One

"Do you want to do this standing up or lying down?"

Lucki Stevenson shrugged. "I don't care. What works best for you?"

"Standing—and hurry. Bend over the table."

Turning away from Sam Kirk, Lucki did just that, placing her elbows square on the table to brace herself. She stared at the back wall of Sam's kitchen, focusing on the sunflower print his mother had hung there years ago, and waited for what seemed a small eternity. She was anything but embarrassed—she was furious.

"You're going to feel a little pop, then a sting. No big deal."

"Just do it!"

Grimacing, Lucki gritted her teeth and waited. Pop. Sting. She squirmed. Yeah, he was right. Not a big deal. A minute later, she was numb.

"All right. It's in there pretty deep, but I can take care of it."

For an undetermined amount of time, Lucki stared at the print while he probed. *Okay, let's get this over with.*

"Hold on. I'm going in with the tweezers now."

Tweezers?

"I'm halfway in. Hold still. I've got to widen the point of entry just a little more."

Lucki gripped the edges of the table and felt the last tug.

"There!"

Sam emitted a satisfying sigh behind her, followed by a definite ping. "There. Got it."

Thank God! "Was that it? Did you get the damn thing out? Are you finished?"

"Not quite. Let me clean up the blood. Douse it with some antiseptic. I think you may need a stitch or two. And you probably should get a tetanus shot."

"Stitches!" Lucki jerked and tried to look behind her.

"Dammit, Lucki! Hold still. Now you've got blood all over me, and I've got a date in twenty minutes."

"Well, la-di-dah!" Lucki rose further on her elbows and turned to look Sam dead in the eye. "At least you don't have a BB embedded in the cheek of your butt!"

He tossed her a sarcastic grin. "You don't either now, smart ass, thanks to me. Now turn around and hold still while I finish up here."

Turning, Lucki waited until she felt a couple of tugs on the wound. Stitches, she guessed. Maybe it was better she couldn't see.

"Thanks to your little brother and his equally bratty friend, I am enduring this humiliation."

"Lay off J.J. and Spud, will you? I'll take care of them."

"Oh, yeah? Like the time they put that mangy old cat in the cab of my truck all night? The animal peed all over my carpet and ate the last of my donuts. You didn't do a thing but make them apologize." She glanced back again. "Do you know how dreadful cat pee smells?"

Sam grimaced and soaked a cotton ball with something cold and daubed it over Lucki's wound. She flinched.

"What did you want me to do? And why do you keep donuts in your truck cab, anyway?"

"I keep them there so I can eat on my way to work. It's quicker that way."

"Most people keep their donuts in the kitchen."

"I'm not most people."

"How well I've learned that over the years."

Lucki stared at the print again. Sunflowers. Sam's mom loved sunflowers. Lucki instantly felt a pang. She'd loved Sam's mother almost as much as she loved her own. Martha Kirk could make the best-damned butterscotch-oatmeal cookies. Lucki grinned. She'd eaten millions of them with milk at this table.

Now this is a twist. Bet Martha expected no one to have minor surgery on her antique oak pedestal table.

Damn those thirteen-year-old, adolescent, scoundrels. When she got hold of them, she would give them a tongue-lashing they wouldn't soon forget.

"I think you ought to take the guns away from those boys."

"I said I'll handle it, Lucki."

Lucki snorted. All she was doing was minding her own business, washing her pickup truck, and the demons had to shoot her in the butt with a BB gun, right as she bent over to pick up the sponge from the bucket.

She'd slung suds and water for fifteen feet chasing after them, but the sting of the BB got to her pretty quick, and then she realized that the damned thing had actually penetrated her cheek, just beneath the leg opening of her bathing suit bottom. Damned, skimpy, thigh-cut suits.

If Sam hadn't been home, she wouldn't have known what to do. Thank God, she didn't have to go to the emergency room. She could hear the laughter all over her office tomorrow. Nothing in Harbor Falls stayed quiet for long.

He placed a bandage over the wound and then taped it in place.

"All done."

Lucki stood and grimaced at the pull of the bandage. She tugged her bikini bottom over her cheek and the bandage and faced him.

Sam continued, all doctor-like. "It's going to be sore for a few days. Keep it clean and let me see it tomorrow."

Feeling a little sassy, Lucki sidled up to Sam, put one finger on his chest, and said, "Doctor, are you just trying to get me to drop my pants again?"

His eyes suddenly rounder than buttermilk biscuits, Sam grabbed her hand and shoved it downward. "Stop it, Lucki. That's enough."

The mood had changed, and even though she didn't know what had possessed her to do such a thing, she drew back and reassessed. Staring Sam directly in the eyes, she lifted two fingers to her forehead and thrust them out in mock salute. "Yes sir! Dr. Kirk."

"Cut it out, Lucki."

Sam turned away and washed his hands. Lucki studied his back. She hadn't noticed before, but Sam *was* dressed to go out, complete with shirt, tie, and his Sunday trousers. She glanced at the kitchen chair beside her. His best sports coat.

"Who's your date?"

He turned slightly and dried his hands on a kitchen towel. Then, he wet the edge of the towel and dabbed some dish-washing detergent on it. He brushed at the bloodstain on his pants and then tossed the towel in the sink. After a minute, rolled down his sleeves and buttoned his cuffs, and looked her straight in the eyes. "Missy Hawkins, why?"

Ugh. Missy Hawkins. You can do better, Sam Kirk.

Lucki shrugged, wondering if she should offer to clean his pants. "Just wondered. You've been seeing a lot of her lately."

"Some." His gaze caught hers, his expression difficult to read.

"You know what you are getting into there, right?"

He stared at her. "Don't go there, Lucki."

She shrugged. "Okay. So don't say I didn't warn you. Where are you going?"

"Dinner and a movie, probably."

"Oh."

He slipped the jacket off the chair and put it on. "I have to run. I'm late already. You know the way out."

Lucki nodded and smiled. "I'm leaving." She started for the back door and then turned around. Sam watched her.

"Tell Missy I said hi."

It wasn't that she didn't like Missy. It was just that Missy was, well...? Seasoned might be the best word.

"I will."

"Thanks for, well, you know."

He nodded and flashed her a wicked smile. "Yeah. See you at church in the morning."

"Sure. In the morning. Have a good time."

Then he was gone. Lucki lingered at Sam's back door and stared after him as he left. Abruptly, she turned and headed across the driveway to her house, the screen door slapping hard behind her.

She didn't bother to lock up. No one in Harbor Falls locked up, at least not in their neighborhood.

FROM HER PERCH IN THE CHOIR LOFT, LUCKI HAD AN excellent view of the parishioners of the First Methodist Church of Harbor Falls. Her parents, Jim and Elaine, sat in their usual pew, three rows back on the left side, two-thirds down from the center aisle. Until she started singing in the choir when she was twelve, Lucki had sat there too, wedged between them like a book between bookends. She wasn't that great a singer, but once she'd realized what fun it was to watch the parishioners during the sermon, she'd volunteered her services to the choir ever since.

Mayor Harold Crandall made a habit of falling asleep just after the offering and the singing of the Doxology. That's why he always claimed the very back seat in the last pew beneath the balcony. Everyone pretended not to hear his snores. If Lucki stared closely, she could see his jaws flap from the choir loft. Ralph Myers, owner of Ralph's Grocery, hadn't moved a muscle the last sixteen years, to her knowledge, sitting stiff and stone-faced as he listened to Reverend Peters. Ralph was row two, front and center. No one at the First Methodist Church of Harbor Falls, North Carolina, ever sat in the first row.

It was darned near sacrilege.

Once, when Sarah Harper's cousin, Sue Ellen, visited from Memphis and plopped down square in the middle of the first pew, the entire congregation heaved a collective gasp. Sue Ellen never came to church with her cousin Sarah again.

Sweeping the congregation, Lucki shifted in her seat and gazed out over the growing crowd of parishioners. The pillow she'd brought to sit on wasn't helping matters. Her wound was sore and itchy. Then her gaze landed on Sam sitting in the pew directly behind her parents. He gave her a knowing wink and a sarcastic smile. She was tempted to stick her tongue out at him but thought better of it. Eloise Hunter, the local piano teacher, Sunday School Superintendent, and the First

Methodist Church of Harbor Falls, North Carolina pianist, had an eye on her.

Dear Eloise always had an eye on someone.

Besides, since Sam had returned home a year ago, she'd felt like she was reverting to her childhood. He brought out the worst in her. Twenty-eight-year-old women with responsible careers weren't supposed to stick their tongues out at anyone, especially in church.

Sam had always sat in the same pew, especially when his parents were living—that is, before he'd gone off to college and medical school and opened his own practice in Charlotte. Martha and Kip Kirk were Jim and Elaine Stevenson's best friends. Living next door, they had shared so many warm and funny times together over the years. Sam and Lucki had practically grown up as brother and sister. It was great because she'd had no siblings of her own. But Kip died when Sam was sixteen, and things changed. Then last year, when Martha died unexpectedly, Sam returned home to raise his younger brother where he knew his parents would want J.J. raised—in Harbor Falls.

The choir stood. Geez, her daydreaming was getting to her again. She rose carefully, the stitches in her rear beginning to pull, and turned to page one-forty-two of the hymnal and began mouthing the words to *All Ye Sinners Come to Rest.*

Her gaze shifted to Missy Hawkins then, jammed up next to Sam. Lucki felt her eyes narrow. She wasn't sure about Missy. She'd graduated high school with Lucki, one year behind Sam, had been married and divorced twice in the past ten years, and clearly had designs on Dr. Samuel Kirk.

Lucki tried to warn Sam, but he would hear none of it. She guessed Sam had lived in the city so long that things like divorce and infidelity were of no concern to him. It obviously didn't matter that Missy Hawkins wasn't exactly an innocent bystander in the breakup of her marriages. She'd scratched her itches whenever and wherever she'd wanted. Sam didn't seem to think it was an issue.

At least he wouldn't discuss it with her, telling Lucki it was none of her concern.

Lucki thought it was.

Then again, maybe Sam really didn't think it *was* an issue. Maybe he was a lot more important to Missy Hawkins than she was to him.

Sam had entertained a steady stream of girlfriends in his younger years, not sticking with one girl for long. He'd parade them past her when they were in high school. He'd bring them home with him from college. All passing fancies. All beautiful, exciting, and they never stuck around. Missy Hawkins wouldn't stick around for long, either. Sam was just like that. He loved women. Wooed and cooed and dined them to the hilt. Then, he'd usually let them down easy and move on.

It was a pattern Lucki had witnessed too many times over the years. No wonder all the girls around Harbor Falls had deemed him *The Heartbreaker* by the time he was out of junior high school. And Lucki, an innocent bystander mostly, hadn't escaped the heartbreak only Sam could bring, either.

But it was just once.

And she'd gotten over it fairly quickly.

Or so she continued to tell herself.

At any rate, she didn't care to dwell on that fact, or the incident, for too long. She rather preferred to forget about it. Because she and Sam had shared something else—friendship. Best friends, they'd always said. Best friends to the end.

That's why she would not make too much of an issue with Sam over the Missy Hawkins deal. She would be gone soon enough.

She hoped.

Eloise Hunter ended the hymn on an off-key note and the

choir sat. Lucki squeaked out a late, *Amen*, and sat too, wishing she hadn't plopped down so quickly.

Finally, the sermon began.

It wasn't five minutes into Reverend Peters' less-than-fire-and-brimstone monologue that Lucki put a bead on J.J. Kirk and Spud Jones in the balcony, perched over Missy Hawkins' head—dropping spit wads, no doubt made from the church bulletin, onto Missy's bleached-blonde, over-teased, black-rooted hair.

And obviously there was so much hair spray Missy couldn't feel the wads dropping or notice the extra weight on her head. Soon, she looked like one of those gaudy, tacky gold Christmas ornaments with fake snow dripping from them that Ralph's Grocery always hung on the artificial tree in the store's front.

But that was Missy for you. Gaudy. Tacky.

Lucki smirked inwardly. *Really, Lucki, you are in church.* You shouldn't be so catty. You shouldn't be so critical. You shouldn't be so—

Abruptly, everyone stood again. Was Reverend Peters finished already? Lucki glanced at her watch. Eleven-fifty-eight.

The thing about the Methodists of Harbor Falls, North Carolina, was that they never held church service past noon. Which was a good thing because the Methodists always beat the Baptists to Buddy's Buffet. It was good Reverend Peters understood the rules of the First Methodist Church of Harbor Falls. Once they had a new minister who didn't know the rules. He'd preached past twelve-fifteen one Sunday. The Baptists got the good tables at Buddy's and had picked over the fried chicken by the time the Methodists had arrived. Harold Crandall only had landing gear for dinner that day— legs and wings—and Harold used his mayor authority to make sure the sermon never went past noon again.

Reverend Peters arrived the following week.

The Gloria Patri was sung, the blessing given, and Lucki glanced into the sanctuary. Missy, who shook back her stiff hair while rising, unknowingly sent paper wads flying like a December snowstorm. Lucki stifled a grin and watched J.J. and Spud exit the balcony in a flash. Lucki mingled a moment with the rest of the choir before she hung up her robe and headed toward the front of the church.

"WHY, REVEREND PETERS, THAT WAS THE MOST meaningful sermon I think I've ever heard."

Lucki stepped out of the vestibule just in time to see an eye-batting Missy laying it on thick to the good Reverend.

Reverend Peters took her hand. "Why, thank you, Melissa. It's one of my favorites."

"Mine, too," she gushed, the lashes batting again.

What a suck-up. Lucki rolled her eyes and whispered a brief prayer of forgiveness. She was on church grounds. She shouldn't be thinking those thoughts.

Stepping up to the trio of Sam, Missy and the Reverend, Lucki interjected, "I especially enjoyed the part about casting the harlots out of Harbor Falls, um... I mean, Jerusalem, Reverend Peters."

The Reverend's puzzled glance fell on Lucki. "That was not this sermon, Lucinda."

Lucki grimaced. He was the only person in Harbor Falls who called her Lucinda. It might be her name on the church roll, but she needed to set him straight soon. "Oh, then I must be remembering another one." She cast her smiling gaze on Missy and then turned to Sam with an arch of her brow. Reaching out, she plucked a paper wad off his shoulder and flicked it away. Sam eyed her suspiciously. She shrugged.

"Well, we better get started to Buddy's before the Baptists beat us," she said. "Coming Reverend Peters?"

"I believe I will, Lucinda."

"Sam? Missy?"

Sam looked at Missy, who stared back at him in adoration, with eyes big as her Aunty Emma's Sunday saucers. "Well," Sam started, "Missy?"

J.J. and Spud suddenly arrived on the scene and parked themselves in the middle of the crowd. "Did I hear something about Buddy's, Sam?" He glanced quickly from adult to adult. "Spud and me sure are hungry."

Lucki frowned. Had Missy just turned up her nose at the sight of J.J.?

He was a great kid. All legs and freckles, a mischievous streak that ran a mile wide, but the sweetest disposition of any kid around—most of the time. He was suffering from a bad case of early-adolescence and a feeling of loss since his mother died. She didn't like the way Missy had reacted to him just then.

"You can ride with me, J.J., if Sam says it's all right," Lucki told the boy.

J.J.'s eyes widened. "Can I Sam?"

Sam gave Missy a look, and she returned with her nod of approval. Damn that woman, she just wanted J.J. out of the way. Lucki immediately bit her tongue. She was still on church property.

"Sure, J.J."

"Spud, too?"

Lucki nodded. "He has to go ask his mother."

Spud ran off. Poor kid, Lucki thought. With a name like Spud, he'd never live down the fact that when he was born, he had a head shaped like an Idaho white. Lucki had to think a minute what the child's real name was. Benjamin, yes. That was it.

"You should have seen Lucki yesterday, Reverend Peters."

Lucki turned to the voice. J.J. was grinning from ear to ear.

"You're heading down the wrong path, kid." Lucki glanced at the smiling child and then threw Sam a warning look.

"Sam had to dig a BB out of Lucki's butt on Mama's kitchen table."

Missy Hawkins' penciled eyebrows shot up.

Sam's eyes narrowed.

Reverend Peters leaned forward.

"Spud shot her with his BB gun," J.J. continued.

"That's enough." Sam's expression toward the kid was stern.

"We watched him take it out. We peeked through the kitchen window." J.J. turned to Lucki. "It looked like Sam had to go in deep. He was poking around back there for a long time."

Sam groaned.

Lucki gritted her teeth and spoke out of the corner of her mouth. "You're dead meat, kid."

"Of course, Sam being a doctor and all, he had every right to feel around on your rear end while you were laying there over the table. Sam was only trying to get the darned thing out. I bet it hurt a little, didn't it, Lucki? I'm really sorry about that. Spud and me think we should apologize. We talked about it in church. We feel bad."

"Of course you do." She gritted her teeth tighter. "And you should. That wasn't funny, J.J."

He nodded. "I know. Of course, you had on that skimpy bathing suit. It was kind of natural that when you bent over to pick up that sponge, that me and Spud would think about shooting you in the butt. It was too tempting. But it was Sam that gave us the idea."

Lucki lifted one eyebrow, then turned her gaze on Sam. Now *his* eyes were big as Aunt Emma's Sunday saucers, and Missy's were narrowed to slits.

Reverend Peters leaned closer, glancing back and forth from Sam to Lucki. "You don't say," he said.

"What do you mean, Sam gave you the idea?" Missy bit out.

Reverend Peters stepped back two steps as Lucki strode toward Sam. "You gave them the idea?"

"Lucki, it was just a joke."

She crossed her arms over her chest and stared at Sam. "What did you say?"

"They misunderstood me."

"What did he say, J.J.?" She directed her question to the kid, but her glare was still connected with Sam's. "J.J., so help me, if you ever want to bite into another fried chicken leg at Buddy's, you'll tell me this very instant what your brother said."

There was a brief pause. Lucki watched Sam's Adam's apple move up and down, and then J.J. spoke up. "He said you ought to be shot for wearing a bathing suit like the one you were wearing. He said it showed too much T and A, whatever that is. And he said if you didn't stop parading around your backyard dressed like that, he might not be responsible for his actions. That's when he went inside and said he was going to take a cold shower. He was all grumbling and everything when he said it, too."

J.J. grinned from ear to ear.

Lucki's mouth dropped open.

Sam threw Missy a sheepish grin.

Reverend Peters laughed out loud, then covered his mouth with his hand.

Missy Hawkins turned slowly toward Sam then and slapped him square across the face—right there on the church steps—and told him before she stomped off, in front of the good Reverend Peters, God, and everybody, that she hoped his slimy carcass rotted in hell. She even suggested that his mother wasn't married when she gave birth to him.

Sam rubbed his cheek and watched her walk away.

Lucki suppressed a bewildered grin and a surprising giggle.

Reverend Peters stepped up to the next couple.

Spud and J.J. ran.

Chapter Two

S am wiped his mouth with a paper napkin and placed it in the center of his plate. Then he opened up the wet-wipe packet and washed the rest of Buddy's fried chicken grease from his fingers. Buddy's Famous Fried Chicken might be greasy, but that's what made it so good. He'd hate to take a cholesterol reading at the moment. Sitting back, he heaved a big sigh and looked across the table to Lucki while she finished the last of her strawberry cheesecake.

How the girl could eat so many sweets and stay so thin was beyond him. He guessed she burned it all off as she worked. Being the athletics director for Harbor Falls' parks department kept her hopping, he knew, but it was the perfect career choice for Lucki. She'd been the biggest tomboy around town when they were growing up. And she was the only girl ever to climb to the top of the Harbor Falls water tower.

Sam smiled as he watched Lucki lick the last of the strawberry glaze from her fork and then glanced out the large pane window toward that same water tower. It was something he did quickly, not wanting to think about the shape of Lucki's tongue and how it had flicked out over the fork. He squirmed in his seat.

Damn. This has to stop.

He studied the water tower. If he looked close enough, he could still see a faint outline of where Lucki had spray-painted in neon pink the fact that Sandra Parker was a slut. He chuckled thinking about it. He was fourteen then, Lucki was thirteen, and he was in love with fifteen-year-old Sandra Parker. Lucki hated her.

"What are you chuckling about?"

Sam looked back at Lucki and smiled. "Nothing." He didn't care to drag up the Sandra-slut incident. Lucki could still get fired up about her. If she knew what Sandra had taught him, she'd probably spontaneously combust. She'd always been too protective of their friendship—and of him.

He watched Lucki slide her plate toward the center of the table and glance to her left where the boys were eating, two tables away. "Spud and J.J. are on their second helpings from the ice cream bar."

Sam looked their way. "They'll burn it off this afternoon." He watched J.J. spoon a glob of hot fudge into his mouth. "The kid has an iron stomach."

"Just like you."

"Used to, anyway." Sam grinned and turned back to look at her. "But no different from you."

"Hey!" Lucki countered, "I never ate jalapeno and butter-scotch ice cream sundaes!"

Sam's stomach turned just thinking about it. "Oh, hell, Lucki. Why did you bring that up? I'll never forget how that tasted coming back up."

"Didn't your dog eat some of it, too?"

He nodded. "Sorry to say."

"I felt sorrier for the dog than I did for you."

Grimacing, he added, "Yeah, poor old Sooner had the runs

for a week. If I recall, that was the last time we played Truth or Dare."

Lucki nodded and glanced off again. He watched her eyes as they played over the crowded restaurant. There was something different about them, something about the color. Or was it?

"You know, J.J. is getting a little out of hand, Sam."

Immediately, Sam bristled. Lucki had hummed that tune before. He didn't know why she thought J.J. was out of control. "He's fine, Lucki. He's a normal twelve-year-old kid."

"Thirteen."

"What?"

"He's thirteen."

"Oh sure. That's right. His birthday was last month."

"And you nearly missed it with that convention you had to go to."

Sam glanced off, watching the boys. "Yes. It was work. What could I do?"

Lucki fell silent for a minute. "Sam, I've worked with a lot of kids. J.J. is screaming out for attention. You've got to put aside some time for him."

"I care for him, Lucki. He's got everything he wants, a roof over his head, food to eat. What more does a boy need?"

"He needs his big brother. He doesn't have his parents."

This was ridiculous. "He has me Lucki. But I also have a medical practice to run. I have to earn a living. I'm doing what I can."

Lucki crossed her arms in front of her and leaned into the table. After studying him a minute, she continued. "Okay, why don't you and I and J.J., Spud too, if his mother says it's okay, ride out to the lake, rent a boat for the afternoon, and go fishing."

Sam sat straight up in his chair. He knew what she was doing, and he wouldn't be manipulated. Raising J.J. was his responsibility, and he would do it as he saw fit. "I have medical records to go over this afternoon and some research I want to do for a patient. I can't, not this afternoon. Besides, I'm not too sure J.J. needs to go anywhere special today."

Throwing back her shoulders, Lucki sat up and picked up her iced tea glass. Halfway to her mouth, she stopped, the glass frozen in mid-air. "Good. You and J.J. need to talk about what happened at church."

"We already did on the way here. I told him how inappropriate his comments were in front of the Reverend."

"They were inappropriate anywhere."

"Okay, fine."

"So, what is his punishment?"

"I didn't punish him."

"What?"

"No."

"What about the BB thing? Are you going to do anything about that?"

Sam felt his cheeks heat. He wasn't about to open that can of worms. It was hard enough watching her parade around her back yard yesterday in the damned strap of fabric she called a bathing suit, and then having to act professionally when she'd come to him to remove the BB—not to mention when J.J. blurted the whole thing not less than an hour earlier to half the congregation. But to sit there across from her, when he knew at some point she would ask him about that comment J.J. made—about him taking a cold shower—it was almost more than he could stand.

What was happening to him, anyway?

He swallowed. Hard. "I'm handling the BB thing."

"How?"

"I'm going to talk to him."

"*Talk* to him? Is that all? Don't you think you might take

the gun away from him or something?" Her voice had pitched higher, and she was leaning forward again.

Sam stood and motioned to J.J. Spud was already heading toward his mother. Then he turned back to Lucki. "I'm handling it, Lucki. Me. My problem. I'll handle it."

She rose, and her tall frame nearly matched his. Looking him square in the eyes, she waited a second or two longer before speaking. "Sam," she began softly, "you better handle it because the problem will only get worse."

Blue. Her eyes were definitely bluer. Colored contacts?

"You understand me, Sam? Are you listening to what I'm saying?"

Sam shook himself, and after a minute, nodded. "Okay, Lucki. I'm listening. I'll handle it."

She threw a half-cocked smile his way then shook her head. Turning, she walked toward the restaurant's exit, and he caught himself watching the sway of her hips as she left. Then he realized—when had Lucki Stevenson, the tomboy next door, grown hips?

The second question that entered his mind startled him more than the first. He was twenty-nine years old. Lucki was twenty-eight. She'd obviously grown hips long ago. Why was he just now noticing? And why was their tantalizing sway rocking him to the core?

"HEY, LUCKI, HAVE YOU CHECKED ON THAT pitching machine yet? Guy Powers said it was throwing a little cockeyed the other night."

Lucki tossed a bag of baseball equipment on the floor next to her desk and then turned to Rick Littleton, Harbor Falls' parks director. "I haven't had a chance yet this morning," she shouted out over the hum of the air conditioner. "I called the company we bought it from Friday afternoon, though. The rep there said he didn't think we needed a new wheel, just that it needed some minor adjustments. He told me what to do. I plan to go out to the ballpark before noon and take a look at it."

Rick scratched his balding head and then replaced his Atlanta Braves ball cap. "Whatever you say. If you need any help, just holler."

Lucki nodded at Rick's back as he retreated from the cubicle she called an office. It was nothing more than an old supply closet with a desk. Various sporting equipment hung on the walls, along with thumb tacked reminders and notices of upcoming athletic events. Sign-up posters for fall soccer were already pinned to her bulletin board on the inside of her door.

"Pinky?" Lucki called out the office secretary's name, whose desk sat around the corner from her cubicle. They all shared Pinky—she, Rick, and Matt Farmer. Matt was in charge of the city swimming pools, picnic grounds, and the playground equipment at the three city parks. Lucki was in charge of all athletics in season—soccer, baseball and fast-pitch softball, basketball, football, wrestling, and even cheerleading, which she detested. If she ever had a daughter who picked up a pom pom, she'd disown her.

Rick, of course, oversaw everything. Pinky kept the office running. She was an absolute necessity to their sanity.

Besides the various umpires, referees, lifeguards, grounds maintenance, and sundry others employed by the parks department, the only other semi-full-time employee was Hazel Green. She ran the after-school and summer care programs. During the summer months, Lucki took the older kids off her hands and involved them in athletic activities.

"Pinky?"

"What?"

"Got a second?"

Lucki waited. She sat behind her desk and rummaged through some paperwork. Where was that damned accident report from the other night? She had to call the insurance company.

"*Pinky?*"

"I said what!" This time the voice was in her doorway.

Lucki glanced up at the neon rose-colored tank top that adorned Pinky's ample chest. Her gaze slid down to the apple-green pants stretched over Pinky's skinny legs. She looked like a lollipop. "Nice outfit."

"Like it? I decided over the weekend to spice up my image."

Lucki rose, trying not to wrinkle her nose. "That ought to do it. Have you done something different with your hair? Oh, and the ladybug earrings really add to the effect."

Pinky's hand went to her poofed, highlighted ponytail. "Really?"

"Well, sort of. Pinky, why are you doing this?"

Pinky's face fell. Lucki rounded her desk.

"You don't like it."

"I like it just fine, Pinky, it's just that I thought your other image was okay."

She frowned. "My other image was boring. Plain. Not exciting."

Lucki eyed her friend. Pinky was an attractive woman, not yet twenty-five, decent figure, great hooters as she'd heard the guys in maintenance attest on more than one occasion. It just didn't seem that she could keep a man interested for long. "Who says you're not exciting?"

"Me. I do." She slid one hip onto the corner of Lucki's desk. "If I were exciting, I'd have a date for the annual picnic by now."

Ah-ha! The plot thickens. "Oh, pooh, Pinky. You and I can go together. You don't need a date."

Pinky grimaced. "No offense, Lucki, but I really don't want to run the two-man, cheek-to-cheek egg race with you."

Lucki blew out a breath and leaned back on the desk. *The picnic.* She'd all but forgotten about it. Oh, hell. "Well, can't say as I blame you. I'm really not sure I can make it, anyway."

Rising, she turned back to her desk, hoping to steer the conversation in another direction. "You don't happen to know where that insurance paper on the Hardin kid is, do you? I thought I had filled it out last Friday and put it on my desk. I have to call the insurance company this morning."

"Oh, they already called. I found the paper and faxed it to them. Everything seems all right. By the way, it was just a broken arm."

Good. Lucki breathed a sigh of relief. That night at the field, they were afraid he'd broken a shoulder. "Well, that's a relief."

"About the picnic, Lucki—"

"What about the picnic?"

Lucki turned at the familiar male voice as Matt Farmer entered her cubicle. It suddenly seemed all the air was sucked out of the room.

"Lucki's not going to the picnic," Pinky offered.

"She has to." Matt turned a smile her way.

"I didn't say I wasn't going, Pinky." *Did I?* "I just said you could go with me."

"No, you didn't. You said you weren't going."

"She's going, Pinky. She's an employee. An administrator. She has to be there." Matt stepped closer and put a hand on her shoulder. "Right, Lucki?"

Sometimes Matt Farmer made her want to throw up. He could be a nice person, but most of the time he stood too close. He was a smiler. All teeth and hair. He was a winker, and she hated winkers. A touchy-feely kind of guy. Touchy-feely guys made her uncomfortable. He smelled too much of Stetson aftershave. Way too much. And she enormously disliked the fact that he was, well, that he was always coming on to her, in a nice sort of way.

Too nice. So nice, in fact, that it was damned difficult to tell him to go to hell. To tell him to give her some space. To tell him he was definitely barking up the wrong tree.

He wasn't her type. Period.

She just didn't have the heart to tell him straight away that he was a great guy to work with, but on a personal level, he made her queasy and half-sick to her stomach.

"I'll be there, Matt."

"Good!" He put his arm around her shoulder. Lucki stifled a shiver. "You know," he bent to whisper in her ear, "I'd bet we'd make a good team in that cheek-to-cheek egg race. Or possibly the chest-to-chest balloon pass. Or even the three-legged relay. What do you think?"

Lucki cleared her throat and stepped back. Matt's arm fell to her waist. Lucki nervously glanced at Pinky, who was grimacing for her. She knew how Lucki felt about Matt. Pinky felt the same way. "Well, actually, Matt," she looked him square in the eyes. "Actually, I... I already have a partner. A date. My... My boyfriend."

Matt stepped back and pulled his arm away. "Oh! Well, I understand, Lucki. I just assumed that you were still unattached."

Lucki glanced from Matt to Pinky and then swallowed the dry lump in her throat. Unattached. That's exactly what she was. And would stay. Except for the weekend of the Fourth of July Harbor Falls Parks Department Annual Employee Picnic.

Ugh. "Uh, no, Matt. Actually, I'm not."

Lucki didn't know why she felt like a heel. Obviously lying had accomplished the one thing she'd been putting off for quite some time now—putting Matt at a distance. There was just one problem. Now she really had to go to the picnic. And she really had to show up there with a date.

LATER THAT AFTERNOON, LUCKI SWERVED HER truck into a parking space in front of Sam's office. She glanced left at his shiny new red Corvette. The doctor's life must not be too shabby, she thought as she slammed the door to her four-year-old, mid-sized, Chevy pickup. Sam's practice was obviously taking off.

Actually, Sam's return to Harbor Falls to open up a general medical practice was a godsend. There wasn't another doctor within a thirty-mile radius, unless you went into Harbor Falls. Most folks in the surrounding area were glad to throw their business Sam's way. And she knew it was all Sam could do to keep his head above water. He was even thinking of recruiting another doctor to join him, and it probably wouldn't be a bad idea. It would definitely give him more time with J.J.

The first chance she got, she was going to mention it to him. Again.

Pushing open the clinic door, Lucki entered and glanced about the waiting room. Muffled coughs, an occasional moan, and an antiseptic smell greeted her. As usual, there was a full house, and she'd forgotten to make an appointment. She approached the window where one of her former classmates sat—the woman who was Sam's receptionist, and who knew everyone and everything that happened in Harbor Falls. To say Kathleen Conner was the town gossip was an understatement. But she was efficient as hell, Sam had told Lucki. And at least, she was discriminating when it came to his patients. Her lips were sealed there.

So, Lucki felt certain the news of her recent, um, injury wouldn't be broadcast all over Harbor Falls. Unless, of course, J.J. and Spud hadn't already seen to that.

"Kathleen," Lucki began as she leaned through the window, "does Sam have any time to see me in the next hour?"

Kathleen glanced up. "Hi, Lucki. Well, let's see..." She looked down at the appointment calendar. "It looks like he might be able to work you in after six, if you want to hang around, or come back."

Six. Lucki glanced at her watch. Four-thirty. She blew out a breath. "I don't know, Kathleen. Maybe I'll just wait until—"

The door behind Kathleen burst open. "Kathleen, I'll see Mrs. Madison now." A harried Sam lifted his gaze from his handful of manila folders. "Lucki, hi!" He stepped into the receptionist's area. "Did you need to see me?"

Lucki thought his demeanor suddenly brightened. "Well, you know, yes. About that, thing that happened to me the other day?"

"Oh, yes." Sam glanced at Kathleen. "Do we have any openings?"

"I just told her, not until after six."

Sam lifted his gaze back to Lucki. "That okay with you?"

Lucki shrugged. "I guess. Either that or maybe I could run over later to your—"

"*No!* Uh... I mean, why don't you come back here at six," he brusquely interrupted. "I'll wait."

Lucki studied Sam, puzzled at the about-face. He looked almost startled. Nervously, he shuffled the papers in his hand as he backed up, bumping into the waiting room door. You'd have thought she was suggesting they have sex right there on Kathleen's desk! With her watching!

"Mrs. Madison, you may come on back now." Glancing once more to Lucki, his gaze darting hither and yon, Sam headed without another word toward the hall which held the two examination rooms.

What in the world was wrong with him?

———

NINETY MINUTES LATER, SAM BLEW OUT A LENGTHY breath as he handed over the last medical folder for the day to Kathleen. It had been a long, exhausting day. He was going to have to get someone else to help him. But that meant expanding the clinic. Another office, more examination rooms, a nurse. It was a lot to think about, but it was going to have to be done, eventually. He couldn't handle this busy practice by himself for much longer.

Not if he wanted to have any kind of life outside of the clinic. And Lucki was right, J.J. needed him.

"Lucki." He said her name aloud. Damn, but she'd been haunting him day and night for days now.

"She's supposed to be here any minute."

Sam turned and looked at Kathleen's back while she finished up at her desk. "What?"

"Lucki will be here soon. It's almost six."

His eyes closed, and all he could see was Lucki bent over his kitchen table with that damned bathing suit on. What little there was of it, anyway? "I'd almost forgotten."

"There's her truck now."

Sam braced himself. The only reason he didn't want Lucki coming over to his house later tonight was because, in a non-professional setting, he didn't know if he could trust his male libido. He needed a clinical setting. Professional. Antiseptic. Cold.

He wished he'd jacked up the air-conditioning a few minutes ago.

He's just have to check her out as quickly as possible and

then get her the hell out of his examination room. He'd thought too often over the past two days what the smooth skin of her shapely little behind had felt like under his fingertips.

The clinic door burst open.

"Wow, this sure looks a lot calmer that an hour and a half ago." Lucki's smile lit up the room, and Sam couldn't help but get caught up in it. She always made him laugh, made him feel good. Always had.

"Yes, and it's been one helluva day. Come on back, Lucki." He motioned to her, and she followed him through the open door back to the examination room.

He left the door partially ajar. For his own sake, not hers.

"Why don't you just drop your jeans a bit and let me look?"

Lucki's hands went to her zipper, and Sam had to turn away, pretending to write something, anything, on her chart so he wouldn't have the image of Lucki hitching those tight jeans down over her hips haunting him later tonight as well.

"Okay."

Pulling on his doctor's facade, he turned around as Lucki was just bending over the examination table. Standing there a moment, he gulped back a lump in his throat as he caught sight of her rounded buns just above the denim waistband. Shaking himself, he stepped forward and pulled back the bandage to give her a quick look.

"Is this sore?" He glanced at her face, trying to avoid her derriere.

"A little."

"It's healing nicely. I'm going to clean it up, put an antibiotic cream on it and change the bandage. Just a minute."

He turned back to the table that held some of his supplies and quietly exhaled. He had to get over this. This was Lucki. His childhood friend. *Get a grip!* This was not some woman he was interested in pawing and getting to know better. *It is Lucki!* Gathering his wits about him, he turned back to her, determined to get through this.

And you are a professional medical doctor, Sam Kirk. Act like it.

In short order, he had fixed her up again. "The stitches might pull and itch for a few days, but it looks pretty good. You'll be good as new in no time." He shifted his gaze first right, then left, and tried to keep his breathing even.

Lucki stood and pulled up her jeans. "Good. I have a lot of things to do. Do you realize how difficult it is to play with my kids with stitches in my butt? I'm afraid I'm going to rip them out or something."

Sam studied her face, relieved that her jeans were all the way on again. "I think you should be careful, but it's unlikely that will happen."

"I am being careful. It's just damned hard explaining to very active adolescents that you can't play volleyball because you got shot in the buns with a BB gun."

Sam started to grin and then thought better of it. *Be professional.* He really didn't want to get into any sort of conversation with Lucki about J.J. and the BB gun. Or what led to that particular incident.

"Are you heading home?" Lucki watched his face.

"I have a little more work to do here, then I will." He opened the door and waited for her to go through it.

"Do you want me to check on J.J. for you? It's getting late. He's been alone for hours. Sam, you really need to get a handle on this. Teenage boys can get into an awful lot of trouble left to their own devices for that long a time."

Sam didn't want to get into that conversation either. Not that he disagreed with her, he just didn't need the constant reminder. Sighing, he said, "I'm trying to handle it, Lucki. I'm going to find someone—"

A commotion erupted in the waiting room. Kathleen's high-pitched voice mingled with an angry male voice. Both Lucki and Sam hurried toward the front of the clinic.

A red-faced Lamar Thompson stood there sparring with an angry Kathleen. "I've told you, he's with a patient," she reiterated. Her nearly two-hundred pound body blocked the doorway. "He'll be out in a minute!"

"I'm here, Kathleen." Sam brushed past her, and she stepped aside. "Lamar, what's wrong? Is there an emergency?"

"You're damned tootin' there's an emergency! I'm gonna break a BB gun over somebody's damn head!"

Chapter Three

Lucki raised a hand and tried to speak. Sam's back was to her, and she was almost glad she couldn't see his face, couldn't connect with his eyes. It would be damned hard for her not to throw him an *I-told-you-so* look. Instead, she looked at Kathleen.

I'm going home. Kathleen mouthed the words and quickly slipped out the back door. The chicken. She knew to *git when the gittin' was good*. Lucki, however, felt she needed to stick around, at least for a few minutes more.

"What are you talking about, Lamar?" Sam's hands were perched on his hips. He shifted from one side to the other in agitation.

"Them damned boys. That brother of yours and that Jones kid that lives just outta town. What's his name? Tater?"

"Spud," Sam said quietly, "his name is Spud."

"Oh, yeah."

Lucki watched Sam's back as he heaved in a breath and exhaled. "Just tell me, Lamar. What did they do?"

Lamar huffed out a breath, as well. Lucki didn't know when she'd seen him so animated. Whatever had happened surely had riled him to the core. His expression differed greatly from the stone-faced statue he was in church.

"Three of my bird feeders are shot to smithereens!" he began. "*Three* of them! Them blasted boys shot them until the wood splintered."

Sam's shoulders fell. "Lamar, I apologize. You're sure it was J.J.?"

"I saw 'em, Sam. Both of 'em. Ran 'em out of my garden and through the alley."

"I'll pay for the bird feeders. Better yet, I'll make J.J. do it. And he'll put the new ones up for you. If you want, I'll talk to Spud's mother."

"I'd appreciate that. But that's not all."

If it were possible, Lucki was sure Sam shrank three inches in stature at Lamar's last comment.

"What else?"

"They tore my Martin house to shreds as well. It's ruined. But what really has me riled is that I found two dead Purple Martins underneath. They killed them, I guess."

Sam's hands dropped to his sides, clenching and unclenching. Lucki wondered if she should stick around.

"You're sure?"

"I've got a backyard full of BBs and two dead birds. What would you think?"

Sam didn't answer. Lucki watched him pace toward the window and look out. It took him several minutes of deep breathing and staring at the street before he responded. "Lamar, I'll handle this." He turned toward the older man, looking at him now. "Thank you for coming to me. I assure you restitution will be made for the damage. As for the birds, there's nothing I can do but offer my apology. You'll get the same from my brother as soon as I get hold of him. Now, if you'll excuse me, I have some things to tend to. I'll be in touch."

Lamar shook the hand Sam offered, dipped his head in agreement, and then left. Sam stared after him for a moment before turning around.

Lucki's gaze instantly met his. He seemed startled that she was still there.

"Don't say it," he warned.

"I wasn't going to say anything."

Sam glanced off and shook his head, his hands perched on his hips again. She didn't know when she'd seen him look so defeated.

"If you don't mind, Lucki, I need a few minutes."

"I understand. I'm leaving."

Sam headed toward the back.

"If you need anything, Sam, I'm just—"

He cut her off with a wave of his hand. "No, Lucki. This is something I have to handle myself. And I guess it's high time I did just that."

THIRTY MINUTES LATER, SAM PULLED INTO HIS drive, barely glancing at Lucki sitting on her porch swing next door. Dusk was quickly falling, but he was sure she sat there alone. It was rare that Jim and Elaine weren't sitting with her. A quick glance at the garage behind the house told him that the motor home was gone. The Stevenson's must have taken off on another excursion.

Damn. He'd like to do that about now. Just keep on driving down the road. But he couldn't. J.J. was his obligation and he had to come to terms with that. Finally, he'd sorted out what he needed to do. He hated to admit it, but Lucki was right.

The boy had been left to his own devices for too long.

The screen door slapped hard behind him as he stepped

from the front porch into the dark living room, stopping shortly to orient himself.

A shaft of light came from the kitchen in the back of the house, along with the clutter of noise from the small television his mother had always kept on the counter to keep up with her soap operas. He rarely watched the thing. He just didn't have the heart to move it.

Approaching the kitchen from the hallway, he came upon J.J. sitting at the table, shoving a ham sandwich into his mouth, watching the TV screen, and bobbing his head in rhythm to the music coming out of the headphones on his head. He washed down the sandwich with a can of soda, then bobbed his head some more. Spanning the room, Sam caught sight of the BB gun propped against the back door frame.

He quickly crossed the room and picked up the gun. Turning, he caught J.J.'s eye.

"Take off the headphones."

J.J. looked at him, scrunched his eyebrows in question, and bobbed some more.

Sam pointed to his head. "The headphones," he shouted.

J.J. threw back his head and then snatched them off. "Hey Sam. Want a sandwich?"

Sam snorted and shook his head. The kid had the audacity to smile at him. Act like everything was normal. Well, it wasn't normal. And he was mad as hell.

"We need to talk." Reaching over, Sam switched off the television. He registered the look of annoyance on J.J.'s face.

"Hey, I was watching that!"

"Not now. We have something to discuss."

"Can't it wait? I was really into that show."

"I don't see how you never heard a word of it."

"So what's it to you? I want to watch it." J.J. stood and reached for the television knob.

Sam caught his wrist and looked his little brother square in the eyes. "Not now, J.J. We have something to discuss. Sit down."

J.J. rolled his eyes and sat. Sam propped himself against a stool at the snack bar. Glancing down, he raked his gaze over the gun still in his hands. "I'm taking the BB gun."

J.J. shrugged. "Where are you taking it to?"

"Don't be sarcastic. I'm keeping it for a while."

"Why?"

Sam huffed out a breath and glanced away. "Do we really have to get into the details here? I think you know darned well why I'm taking the gun."

J.J. lifted his chin and crossed his arms over his chest. "No, big brother, I don't know why you're taking the gun. Tell me."

Sam couldn't believe his ears. The little runt was goading him. What the hell had happened to him over the past few months? Dammit, Lucki was right! His brother was turning into a miniature juvenile delinquent with an attitude.

"Lamar Thompson paid me a visit today."

"His rheumatism acting up again?"

Sam ignored the remark. "Someone shot up Lamar's bird feeders today, destroyed them and his Martin house. And killed two Purple Martins."

J.J. jumped up, his hands curled into fists. "I didn't kill no birds at Lamar Thompson's."

Sam stepped closer. "But you shot up the feeders, didn't you?"

"I didn't do none of it!"

That J.J. was lying really ate through Sam. His voice rose. "J.J., I will not tolerate your lying to me! I know you and Spud did it. Lamar saw you. Said he chased you down the alley. Now I don't want you denying it either. You understand me?"

Before Sam realized it, he'd grasped J.J. on both of his upper arms. The kid jerked away and stepped back. "I thought a person was supposed to be innocent until proven guilty in this country. How come you didn't ask me if I did it? You just assumed I did it, and that's that. Some kind of a brother you are."

The brown depths of J.J.'s eyes flashed so much anger that it was difficult for Sam to form the words he wanted to say, but he tried. "J.J., Lamar saw you, and here's the gun. You've been out today with it, haven't you? And after that stunt you pulled with Lucki...."

"Aw, heck, Sam! You thought it was as funny as we did. I don't know what you're complaining about. You got to feel her up and everything right here on the table. That's what you wanted, wasn't it?"

Something prickled at the back of Sam's neck. He stepped forward and grasped J.J.'s arm. He was straining for control—not of the situation, but his anger. "Go upstairs and take a shower. Get ready for bed. I don't want to continue this conversation."

J.J. jerked away and glared at him. "Hit a little close to home there, Sammy boy?"

"J.J., you better get out of my sight. I'm furious right now, and I don't want to settle this thing in anger. Now go."

J.J. laughed. "You don't know a damn thing about being a parent, do you?"

The comment came from out of the blue. Sam felt a sliver of resentment crawl up his spine. His skin turned clammy. J.J. was exactly right. He'd never wanted to be J.J.'s parent, and maybe that was wrong. Suddenly, all his insecurities about raising his little brother over the past year came flying at him. He'd been doing an inadequate job. He guessed it was about time he started setting things right. Swallowing the dry lump in his throat, he peered deep into his little brother's face.

"Yeah, that's right, J.J. I know nothing about being a parent because that's not what I am. I'm your brother. But I'm also your legal guardian, and I'm about to tell you how things are going to be different around here. First, the BB gun stays with me. Second, you're getting a part-time job after school so you can make enough money to buy new bird feeders and a Martin house for Lamar, then you're going to put them up for him. Third, I'm restricting all your privileges as of this moment—no Spud, no TV, no headphones, no computer, and no outside activities. Indefinitely. From this moment on, you don't move without my permission. If you want a parent, then, by God, I'll be one. Do you understand what I'm telling you?"

The immediate silence that enveloped them both was almost deafening. J.J. simply stared at him, his eyes peering out beneath hooded lids. His expression reminded Sam of one he'd seen on James Dean in an old movie years ago.

"Yeah, Sam. Right. I understand."

"Good. Then get upstairs and get ready for bed."

J.J. crossed his arms again and shifted his weight to the other hip. "Sure Sam. You're the boss. Anything you say."

Sam eyed him. "Then get going."

"Sure."

Sam heaved a deep breath, trying to expel some of the anger that had welled up inside him. J.J. turned, and Sam raked all ten ringers through his hair as he watched the boy round the table—except J.J. didn't head for the stairway as instructed. He headed for the back door. And in a flash, before Sam could react, he was gone.

SAM'S HOUSE HAD BEEN QUIET FOR THE LAST HOUR, but Lucki was still hesitant to leave her front porch. That Sam and J.J. had argued made her uneasy. She hadn't wanted the two of them to have words; she'd simply wanted Sam to acknowledge the fact that J.J. was getting out of hand.

But when the younger brother had stormed out the house, Lucki literally felt Sam's anguish. She was troubled for him. With the slamming of the screen door, she knew nothing had resolved between the two of them. She was tempted to follow J.J., to give him a piece of her mind, but thought better of it. The child probably needed some downtime. Time to be alone to sort out what was going through his head. She'd at least grant him that.

He'd come back about forty-five minutes later, quietly easing through the front door. She'd heard no angry words from either brother, only saw lights turn periodically on or off in the house as they'd readied for bed.

Now the house next door was dark, and Lucki realized she should head to bed herself—but something nagged at her insides, refusing to let go. She hurt for Sam and J.J. and she didn't know how to put things right between them.

The shuffling feet along her sidewalk nearly startled her at first, then she recognized Sam's silhouette in the dim street-light glow. She watched his dejected form slink up the porch steps and slide into the seat beside her on the porch swing. It was dark, and she couldn't actually make out his expression, but as he stared straight ahead, she knew he was about at the end of his rope.

"Rough evening?" she whispered.

Sam heaved a vast sigh and reached over to grasp her hand in his. He closed his fingers over hers and thumbed her knuckles lightly as he propped their clasped hands on his thigh. Lucki had to stifle the shiver that wanted to burst up inside her at his touch, reminding herself that this was Sam. Her friend. Her neighbor. All he was after was comfort. And she shouldn't be feeling what she was feeling.

Not for Sam.

She looked at him. "Are you okay?"

"I royally screwed that up," he replied.

"He'll survive. The question is, will you?"

Sam looked at her then. "I'm not sure."

At that moment, Lucki wanted to reach out and stroke the back of her fingers over his cheek, but she stopped herself. It was just that he looked so lost, so forlorn. She gulped and kept her hands where they were.

"Tell me what happened."

Sam blew out a breath. "He lied to me, Lucki. He said he didn't do it."

"Do you think that's possible?"

He shrugged. "You heard Lamar. What do you think?"

"I think it's probable that he lied."

"Yeah, me too."

"But you didn't make accusations, of course, did you?"

"What?" Sam released her hand and turned toward her on the swing. "Of course I accused him. What else would I do?"

Lucki pulled her hand back onto her lap. Her palm was hot where they'd touched. "Well, for starters, you could have asked for his side of the story."

"Ah, hell, Lucki. He just would have made something up."

"Maybe, but you might have gotten the real story out of his own mouth, rather than you putting him on the defensive by making accusations."

Sam stared into her eyes. "I did that, didn't I?"

"It sounds like it."

"Where did you get so smart?"

"Six years working with kids in the parks department and a minor in child development, that's where."

"I should have listened to you all along."

"That's not the problem here, Sam. You have to deal with J.J. again. And it has to be soon. You didn't actually get anything settled, did you?"

Sam gazed out over her front yard. "Sure, I did. J.J.'s on probation indefinitely. He doesn't sneeze without my permission. No Spud. No gun. No extra activities. And he has to get a part-time job to pay for the damage at Lamar's. I'll make sure that kid doesn't do squat without clearing it by me from now on." He settled his gaze back on her face.

Lucki blew out a breath that lifted her bangs. "You didn't put it all to him like that, did you?"

Sam rose and peered down at her. "Hell, of course I did! The little juvenile delinquent has pulled his last stunt."

Reaching out, Lucki grasped Sam's wrist and pulled him toward her, making him sit down again. She ignored the stirring she felt at the touch. "Sam, you're really an ass, you know that?"

"What?"

Lucki almost chuckled at the amused look on his face.

"You're a complete ass. No wonder J.J. stomped out of the house. You can't treat him like an equal one moment, giving him free rein for months, then pull the rug out from under him and act like a dictator the next! Talk about sending conflicting messages."

Sam stared at her some more. She could see the uncertainty and even the hurt playing over his face. "Where did I go wrong, Lucki?" he asked quietly. "I thought raising J.J. would be simple enough. I provide for all his needs. I'm there every evening, but it just isn't enough, I guess. With the clinic, every minute I have is devoted to something there. I never realized how much Harbor Falls could benefit from medical services. It takes up a lot of my time. The thing is, I know I should be there for him, but it is just impossible to do so. What am I going to do?"

Lucki studied Sam's face. Her heart went out to him. "Sam, look. J.J. is going through a bad time. He grew up without a father. You left when he was just a toddler. And his mother died only a year ago. It's been a big change for him with you coming in here and playing the parenting role, just as

I know it's been an adjustment for you. Being the small-town doctor was never in your plans, I know that, but sometimes plans have to change.

"J.J.'s hurting, Sam. It's difficult for him to express his feelings. And the fact that he's going through adolescence isn't helping things either; you should know that. I'm not so sure that what you did tonight was all that wrong. Probably most parents would have handled it the same way. In fact, if your own parents were here, they probably would have gotten the same treatment you did from J.J. You haven't done an awful job, Sam. Really. Nobody ever said raising a child was a piece of cake. It's hard work. Tonight, you just found out how hard it can sometimes be."

Sam swallowed. His eyes played over her face as he contemplated her words. After a moment, he said, "I thought I was the smart one here. The medical doctor. The guy who left small town Harbor Falls to see the world and make something out of himself. Guess I was wrong. Somehow, during all the time I was gone, you went and got all smart on me."

Lucki smiled. This time she reached out and took Sam's hand in hers, but she wasn't prepared for the intense look that crossed his face. "I've just had a little more experience with kids, Sam. That's all." She released his hand and patted his thigh. A thought flashed through her head. "Come to think of it, that's not a bad idea."

"What's not a bad idea?"

Lucki stood and walked to the porch railing, her hands deep in her jeans pockets. She refused to acknowledge that she had put them there simply to keep from touching Sam. "I think I may have a solution to your problem. At least a start, anyway."

"Yes?" Sam had stepped up beside her, and they stood facing each other as they leaned against the railing. He was close. Lucki backed up a step.

She hesitated and then blurted out her idea. "Let me take J.J. for the summer. He could go to work with me every day, kind of acting like my assistant. Lord knows I could keep him busy. I could get him involved in some sports programs I have going. We have a dirt bowl basketball league for kids his age that meets during the day. Every Friday afternoon we play sand volleyball. And of course, he could sign up for baseball. It's already started, but I can get him on a team. He needs this, Sam. It will get him into shape and let him meet some new kids. And it will keep him occupied and out of your hair this summer while you're trying to work things out at the clinic. I think it's the perfect solution. What do you think?"

Sam stood before her, shaking his head. "I see no reason for J.J. to be with you all day, every day. It's a nice idea, Lucki, but he'd be a nuisance before the first day was out. This is your job. I don't want to put it in jeopardy."

"Oh, pooh." She waved a hand at him. "J.J. will do nothing to put my job in jeopardy. Besides keeping kids off the streets and active in something other than shoplifting, sneaking smokes, and littering the city with graffiti is my job. One more kid won't be a problem. Besides, I really can use the help. Please, Sam. Think about this. It might make a difference."

Sam exhaled heavily, still keeping his gaze on Lucki's face. "I'd have to pay you something. I can't expect you to take him off my hands all summer for nothing."

Lucki pushed at his chest with both hands and then wished she hadn't. "Don't insult me, Kirk. I'm not taking one red cent from you if we do this. I love J.J. like he was my own brother. I want to help."

"Then there's got to be something else I can do for you, Lucki. What is it?"

Lucki watched Sam's eyes. At some point, he'd stepped

closer again. It was difficult to read exactly what those eyes were saying. In reality, she didn't want to know.

A thought crossed her mind.

"Actually, Sam, there might be something you could do for me."

"What is it?"

His voice was way too low and husky. Almost sexy. Lucki bit her lip. "I need a date."

His eyes widened.

She hurriedly added, "You know me, Sam, I've gotten myself into a pickle. I kind of, sort of, told someone at work that I already had a partner for the Harbor Falls Parks Department Fourth of July picnic. I told them that because this guy I work with is always coming on to me."

Sam's eyebrows arched.

"Anyway, I need a date. I'm sure you have a friend around somewhere you could fix me up with, don't you? Just one date. For one afternoon. Oh, and make sure he has some athletic ability because we are going to compete in all the two-man events. Can you do that for me, Sam?"

By the time Lucki finished her little speech, she was completely out of breath. At least she guessed it was from her speech. Sam hadn't taken his eyes off her lips for the past two minutes. "Sam?"

"Uh, yeah, Lucki. Find you a date? Sure. Piece of cake. You got it."

"Thank you." Lucki sighed and grinned.

Sam frowned and then walked back to his house.

Chapter Four

*F*ind you a date? Someone to compete with in all the two-man events? Sure, Lucki, whatever you say.

Sam grumbled and punched his pillow. Three hours earlier, Lucki had said those exact words. *I'm sure you've got a friend somewhere you could fix me up with.*

Yeah, right?

And I've got a castle in Kalamazoo that I'll make you a lovely deal on.

He'd thought about it for the past three hours. Had mentally gone through the list of his single friends living here in Harbor Falls. And one or two who lived in Memphis. But every time he imagined Lucki and one of his friends together, taking part in silly, adolescent games like hip-to-hip Jell-O racing, he got all hot and queasy.

The mental pictures he conjured up figuratively made him agitated.

He didn't want Lucki with any of those guys.

Fred Malone was the first guy he'd considered. Fred, now the owner of the best service station in town and the only wrecker for miles, had made a good life for himself. He'd

45

known he'd wanted to take over his father's station since he was eight years old. Sam could still hear Fred boasting throughout high school, that women loved a talented mechanic. "Service with a smile!" he'd say, bragging that he was the best "tool man" in town.

Sam crossed him off the list when he thought of Fred servicing Lucki.

Then there was George Murphy. George had left for college the same time as Sam but came home after one year of academic probation and with empty pockets. Today, he owned the pizza shop down the street from Sam's clinic. Once, when Sam had stopped in late for dinner, George had invited him to the back to chat and catch up. Sam stood there watching George knead the pizza dough while they talked.

"How do you know when it's ready?" Sam had asked.

George just lifted his gaze and grinned. "You just know, Sammy. Just like you know when a woman is ready." He slapped the mound of dough. "They both get soft and pliable, smell sweet and musky. Feels like putty in your hands."

With the remembrance of that conversation, Sam checked George off the list as well.

And so it went.

Mike West, an electrical inspector, always bragged about being a boob man. He didn't want Mike inspecting Lucki's boobs.

Curtis Back claimed legs were his specialty. Said the longer they were, the tighter they wrapped around him. Lucki's legs were too damned long and too damned tight. No.

Earl Fletcher, a guy who moved into town right before Sam returned, played a little jazz trumpet at *Shaky Jake's* just out of town. Claimed the things he did with his lips could drive women wild.

No!

Finally, he eliminated every single bachelor in town, except for Lamar Thompson. Him, he nearly considered.

And then there was Reverend Peters.

Lucki would kill him.

Sam checked each of his single fraternity brothers off the list posthaste. There were a couple of guys he knew in medical school, but they were married to their careers right now.

There was no one.

Not one man he would trust with Lucki.

Save himself.

Why in the hell had Lucki put herself—and him—into this stupid predicament?

He didn't like the fact that Lucki had lied to her co-workers because some jackass was coming on to her. He didn't like that, not one bit. And that she hadn't thought to ask *him* to take her to the Harbor Falls Parks Department Fourth of July picnic sorely aggravated him.

Come on, Kirk. She was only asking you for a favor. It wasn't personal.

But if she needed some help, why didn't she just come out and ask him to help her? To be her date? Was he not athletic enough? He tried work out as often as he could. Even ran a couple miles a few times a week. Or was it just that she didn't consider him "date" material?

Hell, face it, Kirk. She still considers you the boy next door. Always had, always will. It's time you got thoughts of Lucki and her thigh-cut bathing suit out of your mind. She is your friend, pure and simple, and the mere fact that she hasn't asked you to take her to the picnic confirms she thinks the same about you, old boy. You are her friend. End of story.

But you'll be safe with me. Don't you understand that, Lucki?

Or would she?

Sam rolled over, taking the sheet and blanket with him.

He'd never get to sleep. Thinking of spending the rest of his life as Lucki's friend was a hell of a note to get to sleep on, anyway.

SAM HALF-LISTENED FOR THE PHONE ALL DAY. WHEN he was out of the examination rooms, studying patients' charts and whatnot, he had lent half an ear to the conversations Kathleen was having at her desk. Not a single one-sided conversation showed that Lucki was having the least bit of a problem with J.J.

Funny, his little brother was finally safe and cared for, so he could completely concentrate on the clinic, but he couldn't get his mind off what J.J. and Lucki were doing all day today.

Actually, he couldn't get his mind off Lucki. Any day.

It was becoming an annoying, pleasant, aggravating habit.

But he would deal with that later. Now, he couldn't wait for them to get home, praying that J.J. had not wreaked havoc with the Harbor Falls Parks Department and Lucki Stevenson's job.

The chime over the door sounded. Last patient gone. He glanced at his watch—ten minutes until five o'clock. Lucki should be home any minute. If he hurried, he just might make it home about the same time they pulled into her drive.

He tossed a folder onto Kathleen's desk. "Can you finish up here, Kathleen?"

Glancing up from her work, Kathleen simultaneously pushed her glasses further up on her nose. "Go home, Sam. I'll lock up on my way out."

"Sure you don't mind?"

A sly grin broke her face. "I said, get outta here. You've been pacing the floor all afternoon."

Sam lifted one corner of his mouth into a crooked smile and shook his head. "I'm outta here."

LUCKI GLANCED TO HER RIGHT. J.J. SAT WITH HIS head leaning against the passenger door window. His arms crossed, he faked sleep underneath his narrow, dark sunglasses. His ball cap slung low over his eyebrows. She knew he was pretending. And he knew she knew it too. The day hadn't exactly gone off without a hitch, but she wasn't worried. After all, boys will be boys. J.J. would settle into the routine, eventually. Today was just an adjustment. A petty flaw. A tiny kink in the plans.

It was a minor disagreement between one of her boys and J.J.

Then why did she feel so damned guilty?

Because I promised Sam his little brother would be safe and well cared for. And now...now I'm going to have to explain this slight skirmish.

Or perhaps she could say nothing at all.

Groaning, Lucki faced the stretch of road in front of her. They'd left the parks department, located on the outskirts beyond the Old Harbor Falls section of town, nearly twenty minutes ago. They should pull into her driveway on the south side of town in another few minutes. She'd better set things straight with J.J. before they got there. He hadn't spoken a word since they'd gotten into her truck. And try as she might to ignore the rowdy situation she'd seen some of her tougher boys instigate, she'd had to intervene. J.J. was square in the middle of it, but she hadn't gotten the entire story out of him.

Pulling over to the side of the road, she drew in a steadying breath and punched J.J. on the shoulder.

"Okay, let's hash this thing out before we get home. Sit up, I know you're not asleep."

Lucki waited a minute then J.J. finally pulled himself upright and angled his face toward her. It was difficult to see his eyes through the sunglasses. "I ain't going back there," he said.

Lucki turned to face him. "You most certainly are."

"No, I'm not." J.J. looked out his window.

"All right. Tell me what happened then, and I'll see if I can make some sense out of all this."

It took a couple of minutes before J.J. turned back to look at her. "I don't want to be your assistant."

Lucki dropped her head in a slow nod. "Okay. So you're not my assistant. What do you want to do then?"

"I want to stay home the rest of the summer and hang out with Spud."

"You know Sam has put his foot down. That's not likely to happen. Besides, I heard Spud's mom was sending him off to summer camp."

J.J. snorted.

"Tell me what happened." Lucki waited.

J.J. turned and faced her fully, angling his face more to his left. Slowly he reached up and removed his sunglasses first and then the cap. Lucki gasped.

"My God! Your eye!" Reaching out, Lucki tried to smooth the pads of her fingers over the swollen, bruised eye and cheekbone. J.J. flinched, and Lucki jerked her hand away.

"I didn't see it coming."

"Who did this to you?"

J.J. shrugged.

Lucki narrowed her eyes. "I repeat, who did this to you?" She suspected she would never know. But it was one of her kids, and she wanted to know who was responsible.

J.J. looked away. "They said I was your flunky, your

gopher. A wimp. They made fun of me when I was helping you set up the volleyball nets, especially when I got my feet tangled in one of them. And then they made nasty remarks about how I was playing. Can I help it if I have never played volleyball like that before? Last time I played was in fourth grade gym class, boys against the girls."

"But what about your eye?"

J.J. heaved in a long breath and then forced it out of his mouth. "Like I told you, I didn't see it coming."

"What provoked this?"

"They were making fun of me."

"And you didn't like that."

"No."

"So, what did you do?"

J.J. stared straight ahead for a minute. A slow grin spread across his face. "I called the guy a...." J.J. lowered his voice and whispered the derogatory word.

Lucki jerked back and stared at him, her eyes wide. "And then what?"

J.J. shrugged. "That's when he punched my lights out."

Lucki stared straight ahead and blew out a lengthy breath. Sam was going to kill her. "I don't suppose you could cover up that shiner for a day or two, could you?" After a minute of silence in the cab, she turned to J.J. "Naw, never mind. No use both of us getting into any more trouble than we're already in."

She faced the steering wheel and twisted the key in the ignition. "Guess there's nothing left to do but tell him the truth." She heard J.J. groan and watched out of the corner of her eye as he replaced the sunglasses and ball cap.

———

SAM WAITED ON THE PORCH. LUCKI WAS A GOOD thirty minutes late. When she didn't have activities at night, she was usually like clockwork, almost five o'clock on the dot when she'd pull into her driveway. It was nearly five-thirty, and they weren't home yet.

Something was wrong.

Why in the world had he let Lucki talk him into this hairbrained scheme of hers? It was just that he was at his wit's end the other night. He'd needed guidance, and Lucki had damned near taken the problem off his hands. Only now, the problem was hers. How could he have let Lucki take on his responsibility of J.J. over the summer? It was too much for her to handle. He'd have to come up with another solution.

Maybe he could find J.J. work downtown to occupy his days this summer.

The crunch of gravel alerted him to the fact that Lucki had pulled in the drive, stopping just short of his porch. Both she and J.J. slowly exited the cab of her mid-sized Chevy.

Sam stood and met them near the porch steps. "Hey! How'd it go?"

He watched the brief exchange of eye contact that took place between Lucki and J.J. It gave him a bad feeling. *Damn.*

"Everything went pretty well, I'd say, wouldn't you, J.J.?" Lucki pushed her hands in the pockets of her athletic shorts and smiled at Sam.

"Sure, everything went pretty good," J.J. echoed.

Sam inhaled and stared at the two. "And both of you are full of hog manure."

He watched Lucki's eyes widen in surprise then slid his glance to J.J. He couldn't see a damned thing behind those dark glasses of his, or through the shadow his ball cap had thrown over his face.

"What the heck are you talking about, Sam?"

Sam chuckled. "Give it to me straight, Lucki. Something's

not right here. What did J.J. do?"

J.J. took a half step forward. "I didn't do nothing, did I, Lucki?"

Lucki reached out and grasped J.J.'s arm, pulling him closer. Sam still held her gaze. "He didn't do anything, Sam. Assume nothing until you know what you're talking about."

"Then what am I talking about?"

Lucki bit her lip and glanced at a silent J.J. "There was a slight skirmish today."

Sam huffed, stepped back, and shook his head. "A slight skirmish."

"It was no big deal. It's handled. It won't happen again. And it wasn't J.J.'s fault."

"Yeah, right."

Sam stared at the porch floor. *Sure, it wasn't J.J.'s fault. It's never J.J.'s fault.* He didn't feel Lucki's hands grasp his arms until she forced him to look at her.

"What the hell do you think you're doing?" she hissed. Sam stared into her blue eyes. They were flaring with anger.

"What am I doing? I'm facing reality here, Lucki. You need to face it, too. It was a bad idea. Let's think of something else."

Her fingernails bit into his upper arms. "No, Sam. You have it all wrong. J.J. is not at fault here. And you're being just a little bit arrogant."

Sam huffed out a breath, and then, sensing J.J. walking off, he glanced his way.

"Forget it, Lucki," the boy said. "Sam always thinks it's my fault."

Sam broke away and grasped his brother's forearm, halting him. "Oh, no you don't. You will not stomp out of here this time."

Lucki pleaded from behind, "Sam, stop. You have it all wrong, I tell you. J.J. did nothing."

"Take off those sunglasses and that cap," he directed to his brother, ignoring Lucki. "I hate talking to you when I can't even see your eyes."

After an instant's pause, J.J. ripped off the glasses and cap and sent them flying. His eyes and actions dared Sam to do or say anything out of line. Sam took one look at his brother's face and felt nauseous. "Who in the hell hit you and what did you do to provoke it?"

"Sam," Lucki interjected, "I've been trying to tell you. He did nothing."

J.J. glared back into Sam's eyes. "Forget it, Lucki. He never believes me."

"Well, he'd better start."

Sam whirled back to Lucki. "Stay out of my business, Lucki."

He watched her back jerk straight and her facial expression glare, hard as steel. "This is my business, Sam. J.J. was with me today, and what happened was not his fault."

"He's not going back with you. I'll figure out something else." Sam paused at the pained expression that lanced over Lucki's face. *Damn, why am I being such an ass?*

"You're making a mistake, Sam. J.J. needs to go back. He's got to get back on the horse and ride." Lucki pinned him with her gaze.

"Lose the cliché Lucki, he's staying here."

"Sam—"

"The decision is made."

"No, it's not!" J.J. burst between his brother and Lucki, glancing from one to the other. After a minute, he turned to his older brother and said, "Lucki's right. I'm going back. I will not take those guys calling me a wimp and a flunky. I'm going back tomorrow, black eye and all, and you're not going to stop me!"

When J.J. finished, he was almost in tears. Sam stared into

the boy's face and saw a brief reflection of himself, when he was in his early teens, coming home with a shiner from fighting with Billy Martini, when Billy had called him the teacher's pet. Suddenly, that feeling washed all over him.

He closed his eyes and tried to let the memory pass. Sometimes, there were just things a guy had to do. He guessed J.J. needed to go back. Prove a point.

Sam knew he had to let this go. Apologize to everyone.

He faced J.J. "So you really want to go back?"

"Yes, I do. I didn't think I did, but now I do."

Sam exhaled deeply. "All right. Go back."

He watched J.J.'s lips form a slight smile.

"And... And I'm sorry I didn't believe you. I'm going to do better."

J.J. grinned fully and stepped into the house. One minor victory, Sam thought. When his eyes swung around to meet Lucki's, Sam knew he'd done the right thing. "I'm sorry, Lucki. I've been a bear's ass all day thinking about how you two were getting along."

"It's okay, Sam," she returned softly. "Now that you've made the right decision." She tossed him a wicked grin. "But a minute ago I would have called you a horse's ass, not a bear's."

Sam nodded. "And you would have been right."

When she stepped closer and put her arms around his neck and held him close, and then planted a quick kiss on his cheek, Sam knew he'd won a minor victory with Lucki today as well.

However, when she left his porch to put her truck in the garage, he felt the battle going on deep inside him raging up again. A battle he hadn't clearly defined.

And as far as that battle was concerned, he also knew he was a long way from eventual triumph.

He wouldn't allow himself to consider the possibility of defeat.

Chapter Five

I t was all Lucki could do to keep her eyes on the hymnal, her lips moving in sync to the upbeat hymn, and her feet from prancing nervously on the hardwood floor of the choir loft. On her left, Bess Johnson kept sidling her glances that warned her to quiet her tapping toes.

Bess was fifty if she was a day: prim, proper, and head teller of the First National Bank of Harbor Falls. She sat with her back as rigid and straight as the columns of her accounting books. She despised little children, sloppiness, and men. It was a good thing because Lucki couldn't imagine Bess ever having sex. Too messy.

Bess laid a silencing hand on Lucki's knee. Lucki glanced at her peripherally and ceased the tapping.

She couldn't help it. When she was angry, she couldn't sit still. Her mother used to accuse her of having ants in her pants. And if her mother were here, she'd probably be giving her the evil eye from the sanctuary as she'd done so many times prior.

But she and her daddy were gone, off on another excursion in their camper RV. Any place but Florida, her father had said. So far, since he had retired, they'd done Niagara Falls, the Grand Canyon loop, and trekked down the beaches of the east coast in search of supposed buried pirate treasure. Jim Stevenson was so disgusted with the retired mentality of half the state, he'd decided at sixty-two he was going to eke out the last of the daredevil in him before he "kicked the bucket." And he'd dragged her mother off with him. Although at fifty-eight, Elaine was as spry as the day she turned eighteen. She still ran three miles a day, did her yoga routine before bed every night, and consumed more vegetables than the frozen food section held at Ralph's.

This time, they planned to white-water raft through a nearly unnavigable river in the Rockies, take a five-day pack trip into some long-forgotten gulch, and end up somewhere in New Mexico that advertised bungee jumping and ski diving for the older set. Lord only knew what else they'd get into.

Lucki prayed her parents would make their way back to Harbor Falls in one piece, although she didn't expect to see them until late summer.

The source of her aggravation, however, was not the fact that her parents were out trying to capture the last of their youth, it was the fact that Missy Hawkins couldn't seem to find an empty pew anywhere in the entire church, except for the seat next to Sam.

Damn, I thought I'd gotten rid of that woman last week.

Lucki sent up a silent prayer. *Forgive me, Lord, for saying such awful words in your house. Please. It's just that Missy....*

Lucki shook her head and tapped her foot a little louder against her metal chair. She shouldn't be bothering God with her problem concerning Missy Hawkins.

And just what is my problem with Missy Hawkins?

Your problem is that Missy is too darned attached to Sam Kirk. Your friend. Your neighbor. Your....

What the heck is Sam to me, anyway? And why do I even

care if he sits in church with Missy Hawkins? Of if he dates her? Or even if he takes her to his....

Bed.

No.

Not picturing that.

Something cold traveled up inside Lucki as she realized where her thoughts were leading her. The tapping grew louder as she contemplated the thought of Sam and Missy. In compromising situations.

In his bed.

The tapping echoed within the sanctuary walls.

Bess nudged her hard into a rib and threw Lucki a scornful look. Lucki squealed, then quickly slapped her hand over her mouth. Reverend Peters paused shortly, glanced to the choir, and then resumed his monotone sermon.

Her cheeks flamed.

A few seconds later, she caught Missy Hawkins smirking at her from her seat next to Sam. Thoughts flew through Lucki's head the likes of which she had no business thinking in church.

"So," Lucki said hours later as she and Sam sat swinging on her front porch, "what's the deal with Missy, anyway?"

She turned to Sam sitting next to her, who stopped the swaying motion of the porch swing with one solid planting of his feet on the plank porch floor. "What do you mean, what's the deal with Missy?"

"Well..." Lucki shrugged her shoulders. "I just wondered how serious this thing is with her? I mean, I got the impression that you two were pretty close there for a while, and then after the fiasco at church last Sunday, I hadn't heard you mention her or, to be exact, I hadn't seen her hanging around, so I guess I thought she was out of the picture, but then this morning—"

Sam cupped a palm over Lucki's mouth. "Will you just shut up about Missy Hawkins?"

Lucki stared into Sam's eyes. It was difficult to read what she saw there. Confusion? Frustration?

She attempted a nod. Sam slowly removed his hand. "I guess I just—"

Sam clamped his hand back over her mouth. As he leaned closer, Lucki studied the intense expression in his eyes. "Listen to me," he said rather curtly. "Missy Hawkins and I are not an item. I don't love Missy. I don't even want to date Missy anymore. I never really wanted anything serious to come of our relationship. She wanted it more than I did... Do."

Lucki continued to watch Sam's eyes as they slowly played over her face, watching as he lazily slid his palm from her mouth. His gaze settled on her lips, and Lucki felt an extreme urgency to wet them with her tongue. Her chest lifted in a quick breath.

"Is that right?" she asked quietly.

"Yes." Sam cleared his throat. "That's exactly right."

"Oh."

"Uh-huh," Sam huskily returned.

For a fleeting, crazy moment, Lucki thought Sam was actually going to lean forward and kiss her on her lips. For another sinfully desirous, stupid second or two, she *wanted* him to kiss her. *On the lips.* Then she came to her senses, jerking back into an upright position on her side of the swing.

"Well, then I think you've made the right decision. I'm just not sure Missy is aware of that decision. Believe you me, Sam, that woman is nothing but trouble." Quickly, she glanced off and stared into the night.

Sensing Sam pull his posture erect, sitting on the right side of the swing, Lucki swung her feet and waited for him to make the next move. Repeatedly, she told herself that what she thought was going to happen a few minutes earlier, that Sam was going to kiss her, was the most bizarre, unheard-of thing she'd ever contemplated in her entire life.

Sam Kirk kiss me? How utterly insane. What a joke. Ha! Tell me another one.

Sam cleared his throat. "You think J.J. is going to do all right at parks and rec?"

Lucki, jerked out of her ridiculous musing about the possibility of Sam kissing her, turned abruptly toward him. "What?"

Sam stared. "I asked you about J.J. He really did okay the rest of the week?"

Lucki nodded in agreement. "He did fine, Sam. By yesterday afternoon, he was spiking that volleyball in the faces of the opposing team. He's relentless. But they're all friends now. That's the way it is with kids at this age. One minute they're fighting, the next they're best of friends."

Sam didn't look convinced.

Smiling, Lucki poked him in the ribs. "Really, Sam. Everything is fine. I wouldn't lie to you."

After taking a deep breath and exhaling, Sam let his shoulders drop. Lucki could almost see the tension rolling off them.

"I can't tell you how much of a relief it is to hear that," he said. "To tell you the truth, Lucki, I've been worried about him. I'm glad it's working out. The clinic is taking up so much of my time this summer, and my time with him would be so limited. I don't know how I'm going to repay you."

Lucki smirked. "I do."

Sam threw her a puzzled look. "What? How?"

Facing him, Lucki playfully punched his shoulder. "Have you forgotten already, Sam Kirk? I need that date for the

Fourth of July picnic. You promised me you would find someone. Well, have you?"

The sheepish look on Sam's face registered with Lucki at once. "I... Well, uh...."

"You haven't, have you? Have you even tried?"

Sam's eyes grew wide. "Oh, yeah. Really, I have, Lucki."

Narrowing her gaze, Lucki settled back into the corner of the swing and crossed her arms. "And I'm gonna sprout fairy wings and fly off to Never-Never Land."

Studying him, Lucki fully realized that Sam hadn't lifted a finger to help her out.

"I really need that date, Sam. Please try to help me. Okay?"

It was almost as if Sam bristled at her pleading, although she didn't know why he should be angered at her request. After all, they'd made a deal. Right? And she had lived up to her end of the bargain.

"I'm working on it, Lucki." His voice had lost the easy banter they'd shared before.

He rose and stepped toward the porch steps, a shadow casting over him as he moved away. It was late, the sliver of moonlight in the sky, and the street lamps lining the street, dimming with each step.

Most of the time, Lucki enjoyed sitting on her porch in the dark. At this moment, though, she desperately wanted to see the expression on Sam's face.

"Are you leaving?"

"It's late, Lucki. We both have to work tomorrow."

Lucki breathed deep and stood as well, then headed for her own front door. "Guess I'll see you in the morning when I get J.J."

He waved as he stepped down one concrete step. "Yeah, in the morning."

"Sam?"

He turned. "Uh-huh?"

"The Fourth of July is only two weeks away."

An awkward silence fell between them for a few lengthy seconds. "I know when the Fourth of July is, Lucki."

Damn. Lucki wished she could see his face. Should she reach inside her door and turn on the porch light?

"I know." He took three steps down the sidewalk. "Sam?"

"Yes?"

"J.J. has a baseball game Thursday night. Can you come?" Lucki heard the shuffling of his feet, still wishing she could see his face.

"Yeah. I can make it."

Lucki breathed a soft sigh. "Good."

In the next instant, Sam was gone.

AT PRECISELY SEVEN-THIRTY THE NEXT MORNING, Lucki rapped on Sam's back door. The warm, sweet smell of waffles and syrup greeted her through the screen. She caught a brief glimpse of J.J. wolfing down the last of his breakfast.

"C'mon in, Lucki," Sam shouted over the din of cartoon music coming from the small television.

Lucki entered the kitchen. "Ready, J.J.?" She glanced at his plate and almost drooled. She hadn't realized how hungry she was. "Sam, are those *real* waffles? I'm impressed!" She lifted her gaze to meet his. He smiled back, the hint of anger she'd sensed from him last night gone. Secretly, she was glad.

Sam wore a chef's apron over his doctor's attire and whirled a thin spatula in the air. "I'm a whiz with Mama's waffle iron. Want some?"

Lucki thought about the half-box of most-likely stale donuts sitting on her truck seat. Ugh. "Do you have plenty?" She slanted her head to one side.

"Won't take me a minute, Ma'am. Have a seat."

63

Lucki grabbed the seat next to J.J. and plopped down. The kid was still forking up the waffles. "Does he do this all the time?" She elbowed J.J. in the ribs.

Nodding, he smacked his lips and kept his gaze glued to the television.

"That's why you won't eat my donuts, huh?"

J.J. grinned and glanced at her, syrup running down his chin. "That and the fact that I accidentally dropped them on the ground the other day when we were lining the baseball fields. They didn't get too dirty, though."

Casually, J.J. eyed his waffles.

"You little rat...."

"Waffles coming up!"

Lucki turned toward Sam's voice as he laid a steaming plate of waffles in front of her. Reaching for the butter and syrup, Lucki gave Sam an appreciative glance. "You sure know the way to a woman's heart."

"Really?"

Lucki glanced up from the blob of butter melting on her waffles. Sam stepped closer.

"What?"

"I said, *really*? *Is* this the way to a woman's heart?"

Leaning closer, his elbows propped on the table, his face only inches from hers, Sam stared into Lucki's eyes. Why hadn't she noticed before how dreamy his eyes looked close up? They were the most perfect shade of gray. With tiny flecks of gold. She swallowed. Hard. The waffles were forgotten. *Oh damn. What did I say? I certainly didn't mean....*

"Uh...to her heart?"

"That's what you said."

"Well, it's not like I have any experience in that area, you know."

"You don't?"

"Well, it's just that... From what I hear... I mean, other women say it's kind of cool when men...."

"What do you think?"

"Me! Uh, well... Waffles, uh, waffles are fantastic, you know? I mean, the way the butter and syrup pool in the little squares and... Well, when you bite into it, it's kind of hard and soft at the same time, and the goo just shoots out." Her words were muffled, trailing off and making no sense. *Try again, Lucki.* "I mean, a woman loves...um, waffles are so warm and sweet and sticky and...um, when someone else, like you know, a man cooks for her it's kind of like, well, warm and sweet and sticky is kind of nice, sometimes, and women...."

Hell's bells! What am I doing here?

"It's seven-forty-five, Lucki. We'd better get going."

Lucki barely registered the screech of J.J.'s chair as he pushed backward from the table. The only thing she registered was the amused look on Sam Kirk's face.

She pushed away from the table too, averting his gaze.

"Gotta go. We'll be late."

"You haven't eaten your waffles."

Lucki headed for the door. "Well, uh, save them for me, or something. Got a doggy bag? I'll eat them for supper." Purposely, she didn't look at Sam. If she did, her insides would go all haywire. How dare he look at her like that?

"I'll cook you something else for supper. If you want. Something warm and sweet and sticky?"

Lucki stopped abruptly, her hands frozen on the wooden doorframe. Closing her eyes, she mentally pulled herself together. Sam was trying to get her goat. He was teasing her. *Kidding her.* He used to do it all the time! Stupid idiot Lucki! He was just playing games. Like when he talked her into "practice kissing" when he was thirteen, just so they could get good at it when they wanted to kiss someone else later on, he'd said.

Yeah, right.

Well, two can play.

Turning, Lucki looked Sam square in the eyes.

"I usually like warm and sweet and sticky in the morning. Now later in the day? I'm more of a meat eater, something firm and hot and satisfying. I can really get into that. That is, of course, if you're up to cooking tonight. Don't do it on my account, though. I can manage quite well on my own."

And with that, she left Dr. Sam Kirk with a silly, dumbfounded expression on his face.

Chapter Six

"That's it, Pinky. End of conversation. I'm not going!"

Pinky stared at her in disgust. Lucki turned away and headed for the water cooler.

Lucki knew it wasn't over. Pinky let nothing drop. But the fact that she'd just told her friend that she wasn't going to the picnic after all wasn't open for discussion. She would not go. Ever since she'd left Sam's kitchen and his waffles that morning, she'd been all jittery inside. She didn't know what it meant. It was strange.

Lucki Stevenson didn't get all jittery inside anymore. That was for adolescent girls who were experiencing puppy love. In her world, those jittery feelings didn't exist. It was a damned shame. Love was wasted on youth. She'd heard that said once. She guessed it was true. When those first incredible feelings of love embrace your heart, *consume* your heart, it is the most wonderful, incredible, and life-altering thing.

But adolescent girls don't really know how to handle it. Not true love, anyway. Adolescent boys, either. They get all possessive and testy and territorial as far as their love goes. It smothers. Squeezes. Grips at the heart until it hurts.

She didn't know what was wrong with her.

She hadn't had those jittery feelings inside since... Since when?

Since *Sam?*

Oh, shit.

Pinky shouted her name, and Lucki glanced down at her overflowing cup of water beneath the cooler's spigot. Her hands were shaking. Why?

Because the last time you had those kinds of feelings for a boy was over ten years ago.

Lucki swallowed. The night of the horrible disaster. Her life's most embarrassing moment. The day she'd blocked out of her mind for years—until now.

Until the feelings Sam had dredged up this morning made the memory of that god-awful night resurface.

Senior Prom. Hers. No date. Sam had been home from college for two weeks. They'd spent time together. It felt good. Right. And she'd felt the tingles. She was practically giddy about him. When she'd asked him to take her to the prom, he'd accepted.

She was even giddier.

Then, at the last minute, he'd canceled. Broke off their date. And had broken her heart in the process, too.

The Heartbreaker.

She'd chastised herself for months. Embarrassed that she'd let herself fall under his spell.

Not Lucki! She'd been the one to laugh all those years when other girls had fallen. Yeah, that's what she'd called him all those years ago. *The Heartbreaker.* Throughout junior high and high school when Sam had girls falling at his feet, willing to risk having their hearts broken by—*The Heartbreaker.*

Sam would always laugh, puff out his chest a bit, and gloat whenever another one fell.

Lucki would laugh along with him and pity the poor girls. Practically no female within Sam's age bracket had escaped the charms of *The Heartbreaker*.

Not even Lucki.

Only that time, she didn't laugh.

"What about that boyfriend you're supposed to have?"

Lucki broke her thought process and swirled to face Pinky. "I don't..." Lucki caught herself. She'd said she didn't have a boyfriend. "I don't think he can make it."

"You don't think." Pinky crossed her arms and thrust out one hip.

"He can't go." Lucki glanced to the floor and headed for her cubicle. "I can't go either." How could she go now? She didn't want to be near any men. Not after what she'd finally uncovered, buried for all those years. After all, she'd nearly wiped it from her memory. She had fallen for Sam Kirk hard that spring.

And all he'd thought about her? That she was like his kid sister.

So, he'd sent a substitute. Alan Parker. An already balding eleventh grader who was Sandra Slut's younger brother. Sam couldn't go, so at the last minute, he called Alan to see if he was available to escort Lucki to the prom.

It was both a stab to her heart and a slap in the face.

In the end, she was glad Sam had opted to go back to summer school in Memphis a week later. It put distance between her and her heartbreak. She might have killed him otherwise, once she'd moved into the angry stage of heartbreak mourning.

So how could she go to the picnic with anyone at all? Especially someone Sam had chosen for her? *Oh, why in tarnation did I ask him in the damn first place?*

"Well, you know Rick's going to be furious."

"Rick's going to be furious about what?" The male voice came from the doorway, and Lucki turned at the sound.

Pinky shot a glance at Lucki.

Frowning, Rick asked again, "What will I be furious about?"

Lucki exhaled and stared at Pinky, then slid her gaze to Rick. "I can't go to the picnic."

Rick chuckled and crossed the room to a filing cabinet. He pulled out a drawer and rifled through the files. "Someone die?"

"No," Lucki answered.

"Dying? Ill?"

"No."

"Someone getting married, having a birthday, or coming home from overseas?"

Lucki shook her head. "No."

Rick turned toward her. "Then why can't you go?"

Lucki swallowed. "I... I...." *I can't tell him I don't have a date. I can't tell him I don't want to come alone because of Matt. I can't tell him my hormones are going wacky.*

"It's personal, Rick."

"And the picnic is your job, Lucki."

"Not directly, Rick. It's kind of extracurricular, wouldn't you say? Kinda off the clock?"

Rick turned and stared straight into her eyes. "Yes, Lucki, if you want to get technical, I guess you could say that. But you know how I feel about it, and you know I expect you to be there. You are a salaried employee. You work until the job is done. So, unless you have a helluva good reason why you can't be at the one activity that tops off an entire year of hard work, I could get pretty technical about this whole thing. I expect you to be there."

Lucki gulped. Rick was right, and she knew it.

"Um, maybe I can work something out."

Rick nodded and then picked up a file. He stalked toward the door and turned before he left. "Good. I'll see you on the Fourth. You're in charge of the volleyball tournament."

He left and Lucki turned to Pinky, who was gloating. Just a little.

"Shut up, Pinky!"

"I didn't say a word!"

Lucki headed for her cubicle and briskly shut her door.

EVEN THOUGH HER STOMACH WAS RUMBLING, LUCKI didn't want to think about dinner. In fact, she hadn't taken a bite of food all day long. Not one to skip meals, she was feeling it big time. Lightheaded, she felt a little queasy, and she was getting a headache.

She really needed to eat dinner.

Didn't want to think about it.

Dinner meant facing Sam. And something firm and hot and satisfying.

And to make matters worse, J.J. would not be around. She had dropped him off at Spud's on the way home. Sam said it would be okay.

Oh, Lord. Lucki pulled into her driveway, parked, killed the engine, and let her head fall against the steering wheel. Immediately it made contact with the horn, which blared loudly. She jumped back up, hit her head sharply on the window behind her, and then slunk down into the seat beside her while rubbing the back of her head.

As she lay there, all she could think about was how good those waffles had looked that morning. Then she thought of how good Sam looked. Then she thought about how mad she was at him after he'd dumped her before the prom all those years earlier. And about how hurt she'd been.

Sam thought of her only as the girl next door then. Not a proper date. That's why he hadn't thought twice about finding himself a substitute for the prom. She was certain he didn't think differently of her now. She was still the girl next door. Always would be. Sam would never think of her in any other way.

He'd just been teasing her this morning. Like he had always teased her. She just had to get all thoughts of the two of them together out of her head.

Sam was just the boy next door. Still was. Always would be.

Lucki grimaced and rubbed her jumpy tummy, then closed her eyes. Maybe, she thought, if she just laid here still and quiet for a few minutes longer, the queasiness would subside and then she could go into the house, call Sam and tell him she couldn't make it to dinner. Then she'd eat some yogurt or fruit or something and go to bed.

Yes. That's what she'd do. Go to bed and forget about jilted prom dates and the boy next door.

THE STEAKS WERE SIZZLING ON THE GRILL WHEN Lucki had pulled into her driveway. Sam watched as she drove around to the back of the house, like she did most every day. He'd turned the steaks and watched the fire blaze up as liquid fat hit the coals, then heard the blast from her horn.

He glanced sharply up at the sound and then waited.

He figured she'd hit the horn or something when she was getting out.

Then he saw her lean over in the seat.

Probably reaching over to get something, he thought.

He waited.

The steaks popped and sizzled.

There was no movement in the truck cab.

She was still down in the seat.

He waited.

Something acrid itched at his nose. He waved the smoke away.

He still couldn't see Lucki's head pop up.

Something was wrong.

He dropped the barbecue fork.

Something was wrong with Lucki. My God! That's why she blew the horn!

Sam took off, running across his backyard, leaped over J.J.'s bike, hurdled the hedge, and jerked open the driver's side door of Lucki's truck.

Oh, God. She was passed out in the seat! And she was moaning.

"Lucki!"

He reached in, grasped both her arms, and pulled her into an upright position. "Lucki! Are you okay?" He gently patted her face.

Lucki bolted. Her eyes shot open. Sam had difficulty registering their expression.

"Sam! What? What are you doing?"

"Are you okay? What happened to you?"

Lucki raked a fist over her puzzled face. "What the hell are you talking about, Sam? Nothing has happened. I'm fine."

"Oh no, you don't. You don't look fine. Your eyes look tired, weak. Your skin looks sallow. You're shaking. And you were moaning when I opened the door. You're sick, aren't you?"

"I'm just tired, Sam. It's been a long day, and I haven't eaten. I was just... Uh, resting."

It took only a second for Sam to swoop her up into his

arms, back out of the truck, and head back over the hedge to his house. He walked around the bike this time.

"Sam! What are you doing? Put me down!" Lucki ordered.

Sam ignored her, hooked a foot into the back screen door standing slightly ajar and kicked it open. He rushed through the kitchen and into the family room, carefully placing Lucki on the couch. Kneeling beside her, he caressed the hair away from her cheek and looked deep into Lucki's eyes.

He still wasn't sure what he saw in them looking back at him.

"It's not smart to go all day without eating."

"I'll eat, Sam," Lucki replied. "You didn't have to carry me in here."

"You looked weak." He lied. He just wanted to carry her.

"I'm fine. Really. Just tired."

Lucki raked her tongue over her lower lip. Sam swallowed. "The steaks will be ready in a few minutes." He started to rise.

Lucki laid a hand on his forearm. "Sam, you don't have to cook dinner for me. I know you were just teasing me this morning."

Sam peered into Lucki's eyes. "I wasn't teasing. I want to cook dinner for you."

Again, something flashed across Lucki's face that was difficult for him to discern. His gaze dropped to her lips. Full. Slightly red. Moist. Then before he realized what he was doing, before he even thought about it, he leaned in closer and touched his lips to hers.

That's when the siren went off in his ear.

Lucki pushed him back off his haunches, sending him flying backward, yelling, "Fire!"

He turned and saw the smoke billowing in through his open kitchen window.

Chapter Seven

Lamar Thompson had called the Fire Department.

Later, he'd told Sam that he'd glanced out his back door and saw the flames from the grill reaching up into the trees and was sure the fire was going to spread from the limbs to the house.

Sam was mighty embarrassed when the fire chief burst in the back door to find him sprawled out over the floor looking dumbfounded, like he'd had no clue the house had nearly caught fire. Which he hadn't.

Lucki sat there dumbfounded herself when, after all the hoopla was through, she realized just exactly what Dr. Sam Kirk had had on his mind before all hell broke loose.

He was going to kiss her.

Oh, damn. And he was going to kiss her good.

It would not be one of those brotherly kisses on the nose.

It would not be one of those boy-next-door, you-are-my-best-friend pecks on the cheek.

Oh, no. It was all very clear. He was hungry. And it wasn't for steak.

It was going to be one of those hot, heavy, passionate, *I-*

want-your-body kisses that was sure to curl a girl's toes and make her feel giddy and sultry and desirous all at the same time.

Lucki exhaled deeply, and watched as Sam talked to the last of the firefighters, the grill flames now doused with inches of cold water. She watched from the door as he bid them goodnight and waved them farewell. And she watched as he turned to her and slowly and steadily walked straight back toward the house. Determined. Yes. Determined.

Oh, God.

Lucki backed up several steps. He was coming. What would she do? Would he try to kiss her again? Would she let him? Oh, God! What in the world...?

The door slapped shut, and Lucki turned slowly.

Sam stepped toward her.

The look was back in his eyes.

The same look he'd had just seconds before his lips had descended on hers and the siren had gone off in their ears.

He walked closer.

Lucki glanced at the floor. The toes of his tennis shoes nudged hers. She felt the gentle touch of his fingertips under her chin. Lifting. Her eyes connected with his. Lucki wasn't sure when she'd seen his eyes look so full of... Oh, God, she didn't want to think about that. Passion? Desire?

Had she ever seen Sam's eyes full of desire?

No. But there it was. Plain as day.

"This time," Sam began softly, "there will be no interruptions."

Lucki let him draw her chin closer and felt her entire body moving forward. The warmth of his breath tickled her lips as his mouth moved and captured hers. Lightly. Softly. Caressingly. Lucki melted. Never had she felt such pleasure.

God. She was kissing Sam Kirk. Sam Kirk. Sam Kirk.

The boy next door.

No. The man next door.

God. Where had he been all her life?

Where *had* he been all her life?

Right here, Lucki. Right here under your nose.

Right where he's always been.

It's Sam, Lucki.

The Heartbreaker.

With everything she could muster, she broke the kiss with a gasp and stepped backward. With her arms stiff at her side, she stood solidly in front of him and watched the surprised expression on his face. "What the hell are you doing?" She hadn't intended to shout.

Casually, as if he'd just order French fries at McDonald's, Sam crossed his arms over his chest and said, "Kissing you."

"But why?" Lucki threw her hands up.

"Because it was about time."

"But, but...."

"But nothing." Sam took one large step forward and grasped both her upper arms. "And I want to do it again."

Before she realized it, Sam had dipped his head closer to hers again. No, she couldn't let this happen. No.

She pushed at Sam's chest and looked him square in the eyes. "Sam. No. I don't want..."

Sam swept her into his arms, and with that warm embrace, she knew exactly what he had on his mind. He kissed her then, so thoroughly, that there was not one thing she could do to stop him. It had been so long since she'd been kissed like that.

So. Long.

Correction. If the truth be told, and she was tempted to admit, she had *never* before been kissed by the likes of Sam Kirk.

And that scared the living Hades out of her.

Breaking the kiss, Lucki headed for the door. Without a backward glance or nary a word, she headed home.

Home sweet home.

And way too close to the man next door.

SAM GLANCED LONGINGLY AT THE BACK OF LUCKI'S house.

"Give me a break here, Sam, why don't you? I can't steady this thing all by myself."

Sam jerked back to look in front of him. J.J. was trying to upright the birdhouse so they could set it in concrete.

He grabbed the pole and righted it. Get the job over with, Kirk, and then you can worry about Lucki.

"All right, I'll steady it. Slowly shovel in that concrete, J.J." The boy did. Sam kept his attention focused on his task until the concrete was poured and they had braced the birdhouse with two-by-fours, some rope, and some stakes firmly planted into the ground.

Sam stepped back and looked into the air. J.J. joined him.

Both turned to each other and grinned.

Mission accomplished.

Sam's gaze drifted back to Lucki's house.

It was a little past noon, and she hadn't ventured out of her house the entire morning. He'd seen no lights earlier, or movement of any kind. He was worried. Was she alright?

The way she'd cut out on him the night before, he'd thought she was just mad.

Kissing her! What the hell had gotten into him? He was ready to kiss and paw at her like she was some girl he wanted to get into her pants. Geez. This was Lucki!

He glanced off and studied that last thought.

Hell fire! It was true. That was *exactly* what he wanted.

He wanted Lucki Stevenson. He wanted in her pants. He

wanted in her heart. He wanted her to fall in love with him and make him happy for the rest of his life.

But—what did Lucki want?

Suddenly, her reaction the night before scared him witless.

She didn't want the same thing. Did she?

He'd seen it in her eyes.

But maybe. Maybe she was just scared witless, too.

"Took those dead birds to the animal people at the university over in Greensboro to see what killed 'em."

Startled, Sam jerked and looked to Lamar, who had stepped up beside them.

"Oh?" Sam asked.

"Yep. After I'd left your office the other day, I got looking at those birds a little closer. They'd not been shot."

Sam let his gaze drift lower to J.J.'s face. The boy just looked at Sam, expressionless, waiting.

"Yep. Seems, in fact, that the birds must have gotten into some poison somewhere. Not around my place, but somewhere. Came home to roost and to die, I suppose. Had nothing to do with the boys. Just wanted to apologize."

Sam offered J.J. an apologetic look himself and looked back to Lamar. "Looks like J.J. is the one you need to apologize to, not me, Lamar."

The older man stared, a blank look on his face, then nodded and turned to J.J. "Sorry if that got you into trouble, son."

J.J. looked from Lamar to Sam and then back to Lamar again. "No, sir. Don't apologize. It was me who shot up your birdhouse. I'm sorry."

Sam felt his chest swell. It was the first time J.J. had actually admitted he'd shot the thing. Did he dare hope things were turning around? Never had he felt so proud in his life.

Lamar shook his head. "Fact remains here that I accused you of killing the birds, too. That wasn't your doing." He glanced up to the new birdhouse and then back at J.J. "Got my new birdhouse. Guess we're about through with all this, aren't we?"

He stuck out his hand, and J.J. looked at it for a second, then took it and shook. "Yes, sir," he said.

Lamar gave a firm shake and nodded first to J.J. then to Sam. "You boys do good work." He walked off.

Sam smiled, knowing it was as close to a thank you as they were going to get. He reached out and ruffled the hair atop J.J.'s head. They shared a quiet moment, each knowing what was on the other's mind, then Sam said, "I don't know about you, little brother, but I think we've earned a breakfast bar at Buddy's. What do you think?"

Grinning, J.J. punched his brother in the side. "If we leave now, they still might have plenty of blueberry pancakes."

Sam narrowed his gaze at J.J. "Last one in the car is a rotten egg."

Both took off with a flash.

Thoughts of Lucki fleetingly flew through his mind as Sam raced toward the truck. One task for the day was already carried out. With unexpected results. Now, it was brother time.

Much needed brother time.

Lucki, he would deal with later.

He smiled.

And he would enjoy every minute.

BY THE TIME LUCKI WOKE, IT WAS NEARLY NOON. She'd slept way past her normal Saturday morning waking time. Perhaps, she told herself, it was because she'd been up half the night pacing and watching the lit window to Sam's bedroom across the driveway. And later, watching the dark house after he'd extinguished the light. And then much later, as she'd sat in the dark in her room just staring out into the night.

What Sam did to her body, she thought no man could ever do.

His kisses were pure gold. The brush of his lips across hers made her tremble like no man had ever made her tremble before. The warmth of his body and the power in his embrace were forever seared into her flesh. Her heart ached to have him closer to her again. Longed to feel the pound, pound of his every heartbeat match hers tit for tat.

But—where would all this lead? What did Sam want from her? His kisses were powerful and heady and made her ache for more, but the question remained: *What did Sam Kirk want here?*

She had no clue about his social life in Memphis. Had tried not to keep up with his comings and goings and relationships. Oh, he would come home from time to time and would bring a woman with him to show off to the old crowd and to meet his mother. But none of them lasted. And now that he was home, Missy had occupied most of his time. Until lately, that is. So, what the hell did his kisses mean?

Lucki didn't know.

She wasn't sure she wanted to know.

So, the only thing she could do, she decided, was to keep on going like she had been doing. Keep on living her life as normal. Keep on going to work and keep on being Sam's friend.

Yes. That's what she would do. Friends.

It's just that they happened to share a wonderful kiss last night.

Friends.

Comfortable and longtime friends.

Nothing more.

She just had to make sure that her "friend" didn't screw up her brain with anymore of those potent kisses.

FOR THE FIRST TIME IN WEEKS, LUCKI WAS LATE FOR church. She didn't know what was wrong with her. She tried to get to bed early the night before. She'd been dead tired all day, what with staying up half the night fretting about the likes of Sam's kisses. Still, she'd had trouble falling into that restful sleep that eases the mind and makes one feel at peace.

It was more of a fitful sleep. With images of Sam and J.J. and Lamar Thompson and the fire chief and Pinky and everyone else with whom she'd come into contact with the past week gyrating through her dream-filled sleep.

Luckily, Sam left her alone throughout the day yesterday. She'd seen him arrive home with J.J. early in the afternoon. She'd watched them play catch in the backyard. And she'd heard them laughing inside the kitchen from her own open kitchen window. Cheerful sounds emanated from their home, and Lucki was happy about that. Also, a little melancholy. She was missing her own parents, out on their life's adventures, and secretly wished she was brave enough to step across the driveway and into Sam's kitchen to join them in whatever activity they were up to.

However, she didn't. She left them alone. Telling herself that both brothers needed the time together. She was glad they seemed to get along. And that Sam was spending time with J.J. But if the truth were known, she was scared to death to step one foot inside Sam's house again.

Scared she'd throw herself into his arms and dare to jump his bones.

And she'd promised herself that wouldn't happen.

It couldn't happen.

It would be heartbreak city all over again. And worse.

So, when Lucki finally slammed the driver's side door on her truck, flew up the back steps to the church, quickly donned her choir robe, grabbed a hymnal, and started for the small door at the back of the choir loft, she had no clue that she would meet with any kind of dilemma.

But a dilemma, there was. Sitting right in front of her.

In fact, sitting in *her* choir seat.

Hers.

Sam.

Her Sam. In the choir loft. Sitting in her seat.

And there she stood. All eyes focused on her. Reverend Peters turned in mid-gesture as he motioned the congregation to rise. Eloise Hunter's fingers poised over the piano. And Lamar Thompson's face still frozen in an eternal state of blankness.

She had no choice. Avoid Sam, she could not.

Excusing herself, she quietly slid in front of him and took the empty seat next to him. She didn't look at him. Didn't acknowledge him in any way. She just kept her gaze straight ahead. Opened the hymnal to the requisite page. Stood like everyone else. And started to sing.

Sam grasped her hand and pulled her back down into her seat.

She turned then, the choir members scooted together to hide them from the entire congregation. "What are you doing?" she whispered. "You don't sing."

Sam leaned toward her, a sparkle in his eye. "I just started."

"Well, you're in my seat!" she whispered back.

"So, you've got one, right?"

Lucki glanced down and realized her hand was still clasped in his, and that he was caressing her fingers. Around them, "The Old Rugged Cross" droned on.

"We shouldn't be down here. We should be up there singing," she returned in an urgent whisper.

"If we pop up now, it will look kind of suspicious, don't you think?" He grinned.

Lucki thought about that. He was right.

"Lucki. I want to talk about that kiss."

Feeling her eyes widen, Lucki leaned forward. "Not here, Sam. This isn't the time." She narrowed her gaze then to make her point.

"When, then? I didn't see you all day yesterday."

"Shush, lower your voice."

"All right." Sam glanced up. The third verse continued.

"I want to kiss you again like that, Lucki."

Terror worked its way up through her. No, she couldn't let that happen. "Sam, listen about that kiss...."

Before she realized what was happening, Sam reached over, grasped her behind the neck, and pulled her closer. His lips captured hers in a lip-lock meant to claim her very soul. Soft, so soft his lips. Then hard, hard and wanting. And Lucki, throwing all caution, all reasoning, all thoughts of turning tail and running to the wind, threw her arms around him and kissed him solidly back. She groaned. Pushed closer. He closed his arms more firmly around her and held on while they kissed, and kissed, and kissed.

Suddenly, it seemed the world turned deathly silent.

Lucki pulled away.

Glanced around.

The choir had sat.

The congregation had stilled.

And all one-hundred-thirty-two members of the First United Methodist Church of Harbor Falls, North Carolina, sat watching Sam Kirk kiss Lucki Stevenson like there was no tomorrow.

And like a cherry on top, center front, standing with

hands on hips, glaring at the couple like she could order them drawn and quartered right there on the spot, stood Missy Hawkins.

At that point, Lucki knew she had to do something.

Anything.

She had to show who was in control there. Who had the upper hand. Who Sam Kirk *really* wanted.

Damned if she knew why she was going to give in to this silly jealousy thing, but she had to do it.

She stared long and hard at Missy.

Then without hesitation, she turned to Sam, placed each of her hands firmly on either side of his face, drew him closer, and kissed him again.

With everything she possessed.

The collective gasp throughout the congregation would ring in her ears for days to come.

Chapter Eight

The scene in the vestibule wasn't much better than the one in the choir loft, Lucki decided. She wasn't entirely sure which she liked better. The look on Missy's face when Lucki finally let go of Sam? Or the look on Sam's face when she finally released the lip-lock she'd had on him?

Or perhaps it was the helpless look on Reverend Peters' face in the vestibule when Missy flew into a crying jag to beat no other and threw herself into his arms. He looked briefly to Lucki for help, then tsk-tsked and cooed to Missy while stroking her bleached blonde hair and ushering her into his private chambers.

Lucki suspected that Reverend Peters might have bitten off more than he could chew, but she dismissed it, realizing she had bigger fish to fry than being concerned about the likes of Missy Hawkins.

She turned and took one look at Sam, quickly perused the gathering crowd, and split like a quivering leaf in a thunderstorm.

There was no use hanging around any further.

By noon, it would be all over Buddy's and after that, all over Harbor Falls. Damn. This thing only got deeper and deeper.

"Lucki. Wait."

She didn't stop at Sam's words but kept heading toward her truck.

"Lucki!"

Her hand was on the doorknob.

His hand was on her elbow. "Lucki, stop. We have to talk about this."

Whirling, Lucki pinned Sam with her gaze. "Sam, there is nothing to talk about." She pasted a huge, fake smile on her face. "Wasn't that great? I know it was dramatic, but now you don't have to worry about Missy anymore, do you?"

Where that came from, she had no clue. But maybe it would be her saving grace.

Sam harrumphed. "What are you saying here, Lucki? That you kissed me like that so Missy would get the wrong idea and leave me alone?" He shook his head and grinned. "I don't think so."

She placed a hand on his forearm. "Sam, now listen. Of course, that is exactly what I did. I've sensed for a while now that you really don't want to have anything to do with Missy. So, I just fixed it for you. That's all. What's a woman friend for if not to rescue her male friends from females with claws? It will all die down anyway, so there is nothing to worry about. Certainly, everyone around here knows how ridiculous it is to think we are a couple? We're best friends! But Missy, now, she'll never get over it. For her to think that you would be interested in me, well, she just wouldn't be able to fathom it. She will find another fish soon enough. In fact, she was looking longingly into Reverend Peters' eyes. We might want to keep an eye out for him. Your troubles are over as far as she's concerned, Sam. See, I've done you one humongous favor."

Lucki knew she was rambling, grasping at straws, and probably not making a lick of sense. But she didn't care. At the moment, it was her only defense mechanism.

Sam studied her for a moment. "Doesn't fly, Lucki."

Something caught in her throat. "What in heaven are you talking about?"

"People around here think we'd be a fine couple. I think we'd make a helluva couple. You're wrong."

She refused to allow herself to panic.

"And there's something else that doesn't add up here."

With each added word he uttered, Lucki felt a little more nauseous.

"The performance you put on today may well indeed have been for Missy's benefit. But I think it was because you wanted to stake your claim on me. In public. I think you want everyone to know that I belong to you."

Lucki stepped back and gasped. "Sam Kirk! You don't belong to me. I was not staking any claim! That is absolutely ludicrous!"

"I could belong to you if you wanted me to."

In disbelief, Lucki simply stared. "You are making no sense."

"I want us to be a couple."

"You never wanted to be a couple before."

"Well, I want to be a couple now."

"Oh, yeah, Sam? For how long? You never keep a woman for long. You change women like you change underwear."

She watched a grimace settle over his face. "Not this time, Lucki."

How could she believe that? She couldn't.

"You're being ridiculous, Sam. Past history dictates...."

"To hell with past history, Lucki. I care about you. Deeply. I'm falling in love with you. I want you."

Lucki swallowed. She hadn't had that said to her in a long

time. He wanted her? In what context? And for how long? She had to turn this around.

"Sam, you're my friend. My best friend. You don't *want* me."

"A very good basis to build a relationship on, don't you think? And how do you know what I want? You won't take me seriously. I'm serious, Lucki. I want a relationship with you. Beyond friendship. A long-term relationship. Very long-term, I hope."

Lucki swallowed. Relationship? Long-term?

"I think you got into the communion wine. You're talking out of your head."

"I think you want to kiss me again."

Immediately, Lucki's gaze fell to his lips and something zinged up inside her. Quickly, she glanced away. "That's ridiculous. I don't want to kiss you. I didn't want to kiss you this morning."

"That's a lie and you know it."

"It is not a lie, Sam." Lucki hated it when she lied.

"Did you want to kiss me Friday night? In my kitchen? There was no one around then, Lucki. There was no one there for you to perform for. No excuses, Lucki. You kissed the hell out of me, and you know it. You enjoyed every second, and so did I. You will never convince me otherwise."

Slowly bringing her gaze back up to his face, Lucki felt the panic in full force. He was right! Dammit! He was right!

She had to put a stop to this.

"Sam." She braced herself and looked him square in the eyes. "I...."

She couldn't get the words out.

"I...."

"Yes?"

She wished she could wipe that smirk off his face.

"I still need the date for the picnic."

Where that thought came from, Lucki didn't know and didn't care. It just popped out of her mouth as if it were the thing to say and the topic of their conversation. Thank God, sometimes her brain operated in bits and snatches.

"Where the hell did that come from?"

She shook her head. "I don't know. I just thought of it. Been on my mind, I guess. I gotta know. Did you find someone for me?"

"You're changing the subject."

"But since the subject is changed, have you given it any thought?"

Shaking his head as though in disbelief, Sam took a step back and paced to the left, and then right. After a few seconds, he looked up at her, rubbing his chin.

"Your date will be at Dairy Barn at two o'clock this afternoon. Be there."

With that, Sam walked off, and Lucki watched him go.

She tried to ignore the dangerous feeling deep in the pit of her stomach.

AT ONE MINUTE AFTER TWO O'CLOCK, LUCKI WAS sitting at the picnic table to the left of the Dairy Barn, her fingers running up and down the sides of a large chocolate milkshake. Chocolate was the thing she needed to calm her nerves. Double chocolate and lots of it. And the kid behind the counter didn't even balk when she'd said she'd pay extra for a double whammy of chocolate fudge made with chocolate ice cream with chocolate sprinkles mixed throughout.

Today, she preferred her caffeine in the form of pure unadulterated chocolate. She had a feeling she was going to need it.

About fifteen minutes ago, she'd gotten extremely nervous

about the person Sam had chosen for her for her date. She'd wracked her brain trying to think of anyone in town who he might have contacted but came up with no one. So, she'd decided it must be someone from out of town. Maybe someone from Memphis. Was a possibility.

What worried her most, however, was the exchange she and Sam had that morning outside of the church. Them? A couple? When had he come to that notion, and why did it seem to bother her so?

Certainly, she and Sam were wonderful friends. Best friends. Had been for years. But a couple? As is relationship? As in marriage?

Geez, this thing was turning into something she hadn't expected. And it scared the hell out of her.

Yes, she'd admit, she'd been having feelings for Sam. Feelings that she'd always sort of had, but just hadn't really thought about, romantically speaking. She guessed part of that was fear. And a large part of that fear stemmed from the fact that Sam broke hearts faster than any guy around. And—Lucki wasn't immune to that, either.

But years had passed, hadn't they? Sam wasn't a teenager anymore. He'd grown up. So had she? Could it be possible that they could share something?

Abruptly, the remembrance of her jilted prom date flashed through her. She'd hated that feeling. Hated it with a passion. And just as abruptly, she decided that she never wanted to feel that feeling again.

No. Sam Kirk, *The Heartbreaker,* was better left alone.

Sam Kirk was not the man for her.

Sam Kirk was her best friend. Period.

And that's all there was to it. She had to stand her ground. Firm.

Lucki brought the straw to her lips and sucked long and hard on the chocolate concoction. The cold and sweet and darkly sensuous taste calmed her for a moment. She closed her eyes and exhaled deeply. Nothing like a chocolate fix to steady the nerves. She took another drink.

Yes, she'd made the right decision.

Looking up, she glanced toward the parking lot, wondering when this guy was gonna show. Then something else caught her eye. No, someone else. And that someone held her gaze for several seconds.

Sam stood leaning against a tree, watching her, sucking on his own milkshake.

What the hell was he doing here? Checking up on her?

Well, she'd just ignore him. He could just stand there.

He held no claim on her.

He was simply her friend.

But why the hell was he here?

IT TOOK EVERYTHING IN HIM NOT TO WALK UP TO Lucki, throw her over her shoulder cave man style, toss her into his car, and take her to his bed. She was driving him crazy.

Why, suddenly, after years of living next door to her, were these wild thoughts of making mad passionate love to her, day after day, for the rest of his life, insinuating themselves in his brain?

Because you love her, you dope. You've loved her all your life, and you're just now beginning to realize that.

It was true, he supposed. He'd loved her for years. She was always constant. Always there when he came home from school and in later years when he'd visit Harbor Falls. She'd always been there growing up. Through the break-ups with each of his girlfriends, to the practical jokes they'd play on each other and their friends, maybe a few enemies, to the quiet evenings they'd shared on their front porches, to his times of greatest despair, when his parents had died.

She'd always been there for him.

He loved her.

Now, he just had to convince her that she loved him back.

Just had to make her see.

Slowly, he walked toward her.

She looked up.

Their gazes locked. He refused to let go.

Within seconds, he was sitting across from her at the picnic table. There was a small blob of chocolate hanging around the corner of Lucki's mouth. Smiling, he reached up and whisked it away with his forefinger.

Lucki sat still and let him, her eyes growing wide.

Sam licked his finger. The taste was heavenly. It had nothing to do with the milkshake.

He sat his own milkshake aside and watched Lucki swallow, her gaze still locked with his. Was he softening her resolve to resist him? That was what she was doing, wasn't it? Purposely resisting him. Her kisses said otherwise, though. She was stubborn, always had been. And she would not give up easily on the notion that they weren't just friends. There was a long road ahead of him.

But he would do it. He would convince her they were meant to be together.

She took another long drink of her milkshake and looked him square in the eyes. "Why are you here, Sam? And where's my date?"

Blunt and to the point. That was the Lucki he loved.

"He's here." No use beating around the bush, he told himself.

"Where?" Lucki glanced around.

"Here."

"Where?" Her brows knit as she looked at him. "Who is

it? That guy standing over there at the window holding the dipped cone?"

"No, Lucki. That's not him."

She looked around again. "Then the one over there, sitting on the Harley? Sam, you know I don't like motorcycle men."

"No, Lucki, it's not the Harley man."

Again, her head bobbed from one side to another. Sam stifled a grin. "Then who? There's no one else here?"

"Yes, there is."

"No, Sam, there isn't."

"Yes, Lucki, there is."

At the second realization dawned on her, Lucki paled. "No."

She stood.

Sam rounded the table.

"No, Sam. It won't work."

"Why? Give it up, Lucki. You want me, you know it."

Sam didn't know if he'd ever seen Lucki's eyes so big. "I *do not* want you, Sam Kirk! Get that notion out of your head."

Sam chuckled. He loved getting Lucki's dander up. "You're wrong, you know."

"I am not wrong."

"Let me take you to the picnic, Lucki."

"No, Sam, it would be a mistake. Find me someone else."

"Lucki, honestly, I've tried. There is no one else. I've run the gamut of every single male in town. There is no one."

"Oh, pooh. There are plenty of single men around here."

"Name one. No, name one you would go with."

He watched Lucki think on it. She opened her mouth once as though to speak and then shut it again. After a minute, he let her off the hook.

"Can't do it, can you?"

She shook her head. "Well, but I'm sure you know

someone in Memphis who could come down here for the long weekend. Did you think of that?"

"Yes, Lucki, I did. All my friends are busy or married. There is no one. Guess you're stuck with me."

Her face fell. Sam stifled the urge to grin. She was caving.

"You have to be good."

"Lucki, I can be very good."

She groaned and glanced away.

"Listen, Lucki. I'll make no demands of you. I won't kiss you. I won't talk about our being a couple. I won't even hold your hand. I'll go as your friend. That's all. If that's what you want." He knew she was struggling. He knew he had her between a rock and a hard place, that the picnic was Tuesday, and she had to save face. He knew what her answer was going to be.

"Oh, dammit, all right. You can be my date, Sam, but you listen to me."

Sam felt his smile spread from one side of his face to the other. "I'm listening."

"Friends only, you understand? Friends only."

Sam nodded in understanding.

Lucki nodded her agreement. "All right."

Internally, Sam breathed again. When she turned and walked back to her truck, Sam was still smiling. That woman was going to be his someday. And someday soon.

GEEZ....

Lucki shifted the gears in her little pickup truck and turned for home. Sam was going to be her date.

Sam.

Oh, God.

One whole day. Cheek-to-cheek egg races. Chest-to-chest

Jell-O jiggle. Three-legged races. Pass-the-straw contest. Wheel-barrow races. And on it goes....

She and Sam. Together. In all this mess. How in the world would she survive the day without kissing his face off again?

She didn't know.

If it hadn't been because she was desperate. That Rick expected her to be there with bells on. That she needed to give Matt Farmer a reason to leave her alone. That she was in charge of the volleyball tournament. If it hadn't been for all those things, she would have kissed the whole thing goodbye.

But she'd had no choice.

None.

And now, Sam was her date for the Harbor Falls Parks Department Fourth of July Picnic.

Oh, hells bells....

Chapter Nine

Monday came and went all too quickly. Lucki avoided Sam like the plague. She purposely waited until the last minute before picking up J.J. that morning, impatiently beeping her horn to summon him from the house, then took off before Sam could stop her. Glancing backward in her rearview mirror, she glimpsed his frown as he'd stepped out the back door and watched her exit the drive.

Oh, Lord, what was she going to do?

The entire day, thankfully, was spent preparing for the picnic, so she had little time to think. Little time to dwell on the subject.

Until Pinky interjected.

"So Lucki," she began, "you all ready for tomorrow?"

Lucki grimaced internally.

"I mean," Pinky went on, "you found a date, didn't you? Whatever happened to that boyfriend you were supposed to have, anyway?"

Lucki groaned. God, she hated lying. Even little white ones. "He got a new job and moved out of town."

"Oh, gee, Lucki. That's too bad."

She waved it off. "Not a problem. It wasn't that serious a relationship, anyway."

The door behind her squeaked open, and Lucki heard the din of kids playing in the rec room across the hall. A hand snaked around her waist, and she cringed. God.

"So, does that mean there's still hope for me?" Matt Farmer's breath lanced across her cheek.

Lucki sidestepped until his arm fell from her waist. She turned, smiled sweetly, and returned in her best Southern belle voice, "Matt, dear, I'm afraid there's no hope for you."

He feigned hurt and pouted. Lucki stifled a gag.

He stepped forward. "But, Lucki, if you're hanging loose as a goose now, well then, couldn't you just consider a movie or dinner sometime? Or, hey, I know," he snapped his fingers, "I'll take you to the picnic!"

Quickly, Lucki shook her head and braced her arms in an attempt to keep him from coming closer. "Matt," she began, "you must have heard me say that my boyfriend had moved, but what you don't know is that I do have a date for tomorrow. So, you see, I'll have to decline."

Again, Matt pouted. It wasn't cute.

After a moment, he sighed heavily and perched his hands on either hip. "I'm never gonna have a chance with you, am I Lucki?"

It was all she could do not to shout an emphatic, "No!" but she didn't. She kept her cool. "Matt, I think there is another woman out there who would love to be with you. But that woman isn't me, I'm sorry to say."

"Oh, yeah, and who may I ask?"

Lucki chewed on her lip and glanced to her left. Pinky sat sawing an emery board across her fingernails. Oh, no. She couldn't do that to Pinky, could she?

Pinky glanced up, cracked her gum, and smiled.

Swallowing, Lucki turned back to Matt. "Matt, I'm sure Pinky would love to go with you tomorrow." She continued quickly, "And I know for a fact she doesn't have a date, and she's unencumbered, as they say at the moment, and she looks great in that neon orange tank top, doesn't she? And what do you think about the new hairstyle? Gee, I think it is quite becoming, don't you? So...."

"Whoa!" Pinky shot up off the chair.

"Pinky?" Matt turned to her with a renewed gleam in his eye.

Lucki raced for the door and waved. "Bye you two! I'm off. Got a zillion things to do today. Hey Pink, if I don't catch you later this afternoon, I'll see you tomorrow!"

Then she exited faster than a hockey puck on hard ice.

FOR THE THIRD TIME THAT DAY, SAM DROPPED A patient's folder and sent the contents flying.

"Damnation, Sam!" Kathleen whispered as she pulled him into his office. "What the heck has gotten into you?"

Shaking his head, Sam replied, "Hell if I know, Kathleen."

But he knew. He knew better than anything.

He was in love.

With Lucki.

And tomorrow he would spend the entire day with her.

"I hear a door." Kathleen was gone in a flash. Next patient, obviously. Puzzled, Sam stepped out into the hall and scooped up the file contents. He'd thought they were finished for the day.

"But I tell you, Kathleen," the saccharin sweet voice began, "I have an appointment. I called last Thursday, and you told me to come by Monday at four-fifteen. That's today, right?

And see, I have it written right down here in my little appointment calendar."

Sam knew that voice anywhere. And he knew sure as tootin' the person behind that voice was lying through her teeth. He started into the reception area and then thought better of it. Kathleen could handle the likes of Missy Hawkins.

And she did. She eloquently explained the procedure of scheduling appointments in an orderly physician's office and why it was impossible that she, Kathleen Roberts, top of her class in medical secretarial school, had made a mistake.

Missy Hawkins didn't have an appointment.

Missy Hawkins wanted something.

Groaning, Sam frowned and slipped out the back door.

LUCKI HADN'T SLEPT A WINK. SHE'D TOSSED AND turned most of the night. Laid awake staring at the ceiling for the rest. Tomorrow was S-Day. Sam day. She and Sam. Together. For the entire day. Together. Doing crazy stuff like balloon chest passing and such. Together.

Oh, geez....

And S-Day was here.

Now.

And it was nearly time for them to go.

Why in the hell was her stomach all jittery and nervous? This was Sam, for Pete's sake! Sam! The boy next door! Her Sam. Her best cotton-pickin' friend since childhood.

This was ridiculous.

Lucki shook off a feeling of foreboding. Things were going to go fine. She and Sam would have a wonderful time. Just like old times. He promised there would be none of that stupid couple stuff. None of that, *let's be an item* stuff that he'd been spouting for the past few days. No. It was just Sam.

Sam. Her friend.

Not Sam, *The Heartbreaker*.

Lucki took a deep breath and glanced out her kitchen window toward his house. Where in the heck was he?

She exhaled. Deep.

Everything was going to be all right.

What was she so worried about? Nothing was going to happen. She and Sam would go, have a wonderful time, maybe even win some races, and then they would go home. End of day. End of story. There was absolutely nothing for her to worry about.

Except—Sam was a little late.

Lucki glanced again at the kitchen clock. He was more than a little late. He was a lot late!

Abruptly, the doorbell chimed, and Lucki jumped. Clutching at her chest to stop her quaking heart, she started for the door. "Geez, Lucki. You'd think you were seventeen again and waiting for your prom date."

A momentary panic swept over her.

Naw....

As she laid her hand on the doorknob, she visualized Sam's smiling face looking back at her.

She put on her best smile.

She told herself that history would *not* repeat itself here.

She opened the door.

Reverend Peters' grinning face stared back at her. Reverend Peters, dressed in a t-shirt and running shorts and Nikes. Smiling. And reaching out his hand to her.

"Lucinda? How are you this morning?"

Lucki swallowed. No. This wasn't happening.

"I'm fine, Reverend. What can I do for you?" she squeaked out.

A puzzled look crossed his face. "Do for me? Oh, nothing. Did Sam not call you?"

Sam. Oh, God. Lucki shook her head. "No, Reverend, Sam did not call me."

He stepped closer. "I'm sure in all the confusion he forgot. But no matter, I'll explain on the way to the picnic. Are you ready?"

"Ready?"

"Yes, Lucinda. For the picnic."

Lucki mentally got a grip. *No. No. No.* This wasn't happening.

"The picnic?"

The good Reverend paused before speaking again. "Lucki, Sam couldn't make it. Was called away on an emergency. I happened to see him, and was available this afternoon, so he asked me to take his place. He assured me you would understand. I know, I'm not the most athletic person in the world, but I'm game and don't mind making a fool out of myself. Sam said you just needed a partner, really, just a technicality. So, Lucki, I'm your man."

My man.

But it was the wrong man.

Speechless, she just stood there.

What could she say?

She had no choice. She had to go. And at least Reverend Peters was a warm body who could be her partner.

But inside, she was fuming. Just fuming.

Who the hell did Sam Kirk think he was, anyway?

"Emergency, huh?" were the first words that popped out of her mouth.

She stepped out onto the porch and hurried toward the steps.

"Why, yes, Lucinda. One of his patients. The Hawkins girl. Some type of emergency."

Lucki stopped cold at the edge of the porch.

The next time she saw Sam Kirk, she was going to kill him.

Kill. Him. Dead.

"Missy, I'm telling you, you don't have malaria."

"But Sam..." Missy lifted a weak hand to her mouth and coughed delicately. "I read the symptoms in the medical book, and I know I have malaria."

"You read too much. I promise you. You don't have malaria."

Missy thrust herself into a coughing jag. "Well, then it must be tuberculosis."

Sam crossed his arms over his chest. What the hell was wrong with him? When Reverend Peters had shown up on his doorstep, urging him to go see Missy, he should have known, right then and there, that this was one of Missy's ploys to get his attention.

But Reverend Peters had looked concerned. Said Missy was in awful shape. And you think you can believe a preacher, right? Of course, Missy could snow a preacher into taking a peek into Hell, if she wanted. She was that persuasive.

"Don't joke about something like that, Missy. You don't have tuberculosis."

"But how do you know for sure?" She batted both eyelids expertly. God, what had he ever seen in those fake lashes?

"We do tests to know for sure. But, Missy, the odds of you having tuberculosis are, well, let's just say they are mighty slim. You've got the flu, I suspect. Your common, ordinary, garden variety flu. Nothing more, nothing less."

"Swine flu? Oh. My. God!"

Oh hell. "No, Missy. You do not have swine flu. I assure you of that fact." He doubted she even had the flu at all, had probably heated her thermometer up on a light bulb or something.

Missy slunk down deeper into her covers, throwing her arms over her head. "Oh, Sam..."

He stood. He knew that bedroom look.

"Stop it, Missy."

"Sam... Could it be diphtheria?"

Closing his eyes at the absurdity of her question, Sam vigorously shook his head. He leaned closer and looked deliberately into her eyes. "Missy, you don't have diphtheria, malaria, or tuberculosis. You have the flu." If that, he thought. He suspected she had more than the garden variety case of sexual deprivation. She wanted it. Bad. And she will stoop pretty low for it.

She moaned. "Sam, darling, I really don't feel so good. Why don't you crawl in here beside me and keep me warm? I'm shivering all over."

Bingo! Could he call a kettle black?

Two months ago, he wouldn't have given the invitation a second thought. Two months ago, since leaving Memphis, he was desperate for female companionship. Two months ago, Missy Hawkins looked pretty damned good to him.

But at present, the sight of her sickened him to the core.

Missy Hawkins' bed was *not* where he wanted to be.

If he wanted in anyone's bed, it was Lucki's.

Or, better yet, he wanted Lucki in *his* bed.

Forever.

He took several steps in reverse.

"Missy, drink plenty of fluids, get lots of rest, eat when you feel like it, take something for the fever, and call the office tomorrow for an appointment if you don't feel better."

Then he turned tail and exited her bedroom door, a tremendous sigh of relief escaping his lips.

By the time they'd reached the picnic area, Lucki was fuming. Shades of the past infected her thoughts. Damn. How could she have been so stupid? So blind? So naïve to think that Sam would be there for her?

All she'd wanted was one afternoon. A date. He'd insisted he be the one. Okay, then she'd agreed. That's all she'd wanted from him. One afternoon. And now?

And now this? Dumped again? And it wasn't even an actual date?

Obviously, Sam Kirk had a lot to learn about women. No wonder he hadn't found a wife yet!

But—what should she expect? Sam was Sam. Carefree. Live for the moment. One girl this week, one girl next week.

The Heartbreaker.

Dammit!

Thank God, she'd not allowed herself to get too caught up in him this time. Thank God, she had not lost her head and fallen for him again.

That, clearly, would never happen.

Sheesh....

This, was a total blessing in disguise.

Certainly, there were other fish in the sea. Right?

As she pulled into the parking lot behind the ball fields, Lucki gave the good Reverend a quick glance. He was a nice enough guy. Polite. Clean-shaven. Intelligent. Probably a great catch for some woman someday.

But not for her.

The wrong fish.

Then for who, Lucki? Who?

Why after all these years, had there not been a man to attract her attention? One to spark something inside of her and hold on for a long-term relationship? Why, would she not let herself get entangled in a man's life and make him her own?

An image of a smiling Sam burned itself into her brain.

"Ohmigosh."

"What Lucinda?"

Lucki quickly jerked her gaze away from the Reverend. "Oh, nothing. Was just thinking out loud. I've got a lot of stuff to do before we get started."

"Oh, I see." He nodded then exited the truck.

Lucki let her head fall onto the steering wheel. Sam's image was still burned into her mind.

She loved him.

All these years, she'd been comparing every man she'd ever met to Sam.

She loved him.

And he loved her.

Or so he said.

What the heck was she going to do about all of this?

Chapter Ten

They made it through the three-legged race.

They fumbled through the hard-boiled-egg-on-a-spoon pass.

They slid through the greased pig chase.

And Reverend Peters broke his leg in the wheelbarrow race, not two hours into the day. Lucki didn't know how she had accomplished that feat, but she knew it was her fault. Could she help it if she tripped over a stick and fell over the man, twisting his leg in the process? Could she help it if he was just a tad shorter than her and her Amazon body and long legs just kind of tangled up over him and his leg just snapped?

Geez, maybe he should drink more milk. Maybe he had a calcium deficiency or something and had brittle bones. Maybe, just maybe, it wasn't entirely her fault.

But it was.

That's why she'd ridden in the ambulance with him to the hospital. That's why she'd stayed until someone else came to be with him. He'd asked a nurse to call a friend of his, he'd told her, and that it wasn't necessary for her to hang around. Particularly since she had obligations at the picnic. But Lucki felt it was her duty to stay until she knew he was going to be okay, and until someone came from Harbor Falls to take him home.

So, she waited.

It was almost an hour before anyone arrived.

And when the good Reverend's friend stepped through the double swinging doors of the ER, Lucki just about dropped her jaw.

There stood Missy Hawkins in all her glory. Hair teased. Made up to perfection. Nails polished and shining. Dressed to kill.

Nice way to pick up your preacher from an accident.

Lucki decided she wouldn't let her thoughts go there.

Standing, Lucki approached her, just out of earshot of Reverend Peters. "Well, well, Missy. I do believe you look lovely this afternoon."

Missy smirked. "You may leave now, Lucki. I'm here. I'll take care of Rock."

Rock. *Rock?*

Lucki hadn't even realized Reverend Peters had a first name. Kind of like when you realize your teachers actually go to the bathroom. It was something she'd never considered. *But Rock?*

"Well, Missy, I'm sure you have plenty of experience taking care of... *Rocks.*"

Oh, hell. Where in the world did that come from? Lucki braced herself.

Missy narrowed her gaze. "Better go mind your own business, Lucki. You might want to take care of what's at home, yourself, deary."

Lucki had a sneaking suspicion she knew where this was heading. "At home? Whatever could you mean?"

Missy glanced at her nails. Flicked a piece of lint from her tight sweater. "Oh, well, perhaps I should say, what's next door then."

"Get to the point."

Missy yawned. "Well, honey, after witnessing that kiss in church the other day, I was just sure you were giving Sam all he needed in bed. But then, after this morning, well, I have to wonder."

No, she wasn't going there. She would not let Missy suck her into questioning what had happened this morning. She would not fall into the jealousy trap. She would not—

"So what the hell happened this morning, Missy?"

Cocking her head to one side, Missy studied her, then finally replied, "I'm sorry to have to tell you this, Lucki, but Sam just left my bed. In fact, he's been with me all morning. I just thought you should know."

Lucki swallowed every ounce of green-eyed monster jealousy that dared to rear its ugly, gnarled head in her presence. She would not, repeat *not* fall into this. She knew the kind of woman Missy was.

She also knew the kind of man Sam was.

Oh, hell....

Lucki threw the most sickeningly sweet smile she could muster Missy's way. "Is that a fact."

"Oh, yes, dear. That, is a fact."

"Hmmm...."

"You don't believe me?" Missy batted those damn eyes again.

Lucki smirked. "Of course, Missy! I just feel sorry for poor Sam."

"Sorry?"

"Umhmm...."

"Why?"

"Oh, no particular reason, Missy, I just feel sorry for him."

And then, Lucki turned and left through the swinging doors. As she headed toward the parking lot, she heard Missy shout from behind her.

"Sorry? Why sorry...?"

Lucki knew that curiosity would eat Missy alive. Good. She deserved it.

And as for Sam, well, by the time she got through with him, he would be less than dog meat.

SAM TURNED INTO THE HOSPITAL PARKING LOT JUST as he saw Lucki exit the emergency room doors. Damn. She looked madder than an old red hen.

When he'd finally made it to the picnic, searched for her with no avail, and then had overheard the conversation about the good Reverend breaking his leg, he'd inquired as to Lucki's whereabouts. That's when the pony-tailed blonde called Pinky, who was wearing an obnoxious chartreuse tank top, told him she'd accompanied Reverend Peters to the hospital.

Pinky also asked if he would be so kind as to fetch Lucki and bring her back to the park, if the good Reverend were okay. Sam had kindly obliged.

He couldn't wait to see her. He knew, beyond any doubt, that he had to convince Lucki of his love. Observing the fakeness of Missy Hawkins this morning led him straight to the conclusion he'd been looking for—Lucki was the real thing. Had been the real thing. *Always was* the real thing.

And he wanted the real thing for himself.

He slowed down and pulled up next to her, and was met with a scowl. No matter. Soon he'd put a smile there.

He powered down the window, then leaned toward the passenger side and flipped open the door.

"Hi Lucki! Boy, that was timing. Get in, and I'll take you back to the picnic."

She quickly slid inside, then slammed the car door. A

distinct frown settled upon her face. She sat stone still, staring straight ahead. "Take me to my truck."

Sam stared at her. *Uh-oh.*

"But aren't you going back to the picnic? Pinky says they need you."

"They can manage just fine without me. Take me to my truck."

Sam tried not to panic at the bitter tone of her voice. "Lucki? How is Reverend Peters?"

"Fine."

Sam eased his foot onto the accelerator and started out of the parking lot. "Bad break?"

"Bad enough."

"Will he be okay?"

"He'll survive."

"Did anyone come for him?"

She turned her head and glared.

Oh, boy. Things weren't going well here.

Sam concentrated on turning back onto the highway and heading toward the park. The icy atmosphere inside his car took a downward plunge. Oh, hell, what had he done now?

"Reverend Peters is just fine, Sam. The break will heal in time. Yes, someone came for him. Someone you know very well. Someone with whom you spent an intimate morning, as I understand it. Someone who caused you to break our date. And for that, I will never forgive you."

She said it so coolly, so nonchalantly, it gave him cause for concern. Sam swallowed down the panic that rushed up his throat, braked harshly, then pulled off the road into the nearest parking lot. He killed the engine.

"Lucki, look...."

"No, Sam. You look. If you want Missy, then fine. Just don't come to me after you've been with her. In fact, don't come to me at all. Don't talk about our being a couple. Don't talk about kissing me anymore. And don't send substitutions for dates with me. Ever. You understand that?"

Taken aback, Sam stared at her. "What?"

"Don't play dumb, Sam. I hate that. You know what I'm talking about."

He shook his head. "I do not know what you are talking about."

"Oh, yes, you do."

"Tell me, Lucki."

"I shouldn't have to."

"Stop playing games here and spill it. What's on your mind?"

If he weren't mistaken, he would swear there were tiny tears welling up in Lucki's eyes. Had he ever seen Lucki cry before? His heart swelled. "Lucki, what's bothering you?"

"You were with Missy this morning."

He nodded. "Yes, that's true."

She turned away.

"Reverend Peters told you there was an emergency, right?"

"Oh, yeah, some emergency, Sam. Don't give me that crap and don't lie to me."

"I'm not lying, Lucki. Missy was ill. Or thought she was anyway."

She turned back and looked at him, her eyes all ablaze. "Like hell! I'm no fool, Sam. I just saw her! Dressed to the nines. A body to die for. All made up. Gloating about spending the morning in bed with you."

"Whoa!" Sam put up his hands. "Whoa! Stop right there. I did not spend the morning in bed with Missy." His stomach turned.

"Oh, so she lied?"

Sam again nodded. "Yes, Lucki, she lied."

"You expect me to believe that?"

"Yes, Lucki, I do. Missy lied about that, and she lied about being sick."

She opened her mouth and then closed it.

"Lucki," he began softly. "Who do you believe? Me, your best friend, who has never lied to you? Or Missy Hawkins, who hasn't the greatest reputation in town for honesty."

He watched her think about that one.

After a moment, she nodded slightly. "I believe you, Sam."

Torrential relief washed over him. "Let me tell you what happened." After a minute, he'd relayed the entire story. He could sense Lucky mentally relaxing.

"So, it was another of Missy's tricks. I didn't intentionally back out of my commitment to you this morning. I wouldn't do that, Lucki. Hell, I've been trying to woo you for the past few days. Why would I pull a crazy stunt like that?"

Lucki shook her head and glanced away. Her eyes still misted with tears. "I don't know," she said. "I wasn't thinking straight."

"Lucki, I think you know how I feel about you. I've said that often enough lately. Let's start over today."

She looked at him, square in the eye, and held the connection for a while. "Sam," she began, "just let me say one more thing."

"Okay."

"I have to say this, have to clear this up, before I can go any further with anything between us."

"Okay, Lucki."

"I want you to know how much it hurt me when you dumped me at my Senior Prom. I want you to know how much it hurt today when I saw Reverend Peters standing there this morning on my porch, telling me you'd sent him instead of you. I want you to know that I never want to feel that again. Do you understand me?"

Sam let her words soak in a minute. Senior Prom? Vague memories slipped through his mind. Oh, hell....

"Lucki, I don't know what to say. Are you still upset about that?" Actually, he'd never known whether or not she was upset. He'd never talked to her about it.

She glanced away. Looking irritated. "Let's get back to the picnic, Sam. Forget it."

"Lucki, we need to talk about this."

"Another time, Sam. I'm not up to it. Let's go."

Sam hesitated, watching her profile, and then dropped it. Huh. Obviously, there was something Lucki was hiding. Holding back. Something that had been bothering her for a long time. And even more obviously, he was going to have a lot more wooing to do before he won her.

This thing was bigger than the incident with Missy Hawkins this morning.

He'd hurt her. A long time ago. And she didn't trust him now.

That, was a problem.

IT WAS DIFFICULT TO KNOW EXACTLY WHAT SHE WAS feeling. That she'd gotten a couple of things off her chest felt great. The fact that she'd actually spoken words about that prom thing felt doubly good. But somehow, she had also felt silly bringing up something that had happened so long ago. It seemed juvenile somehow. So high school. So immature.

Damn. She was a grown woman. She should be able to get over stuff like that. Shouldn't have even brought it up. He was going to think her an over-grown adolescent.

Well, just let him. There was nothing she could do about it now. Fact remained, it had hurt her. And she was glad he'd gone back to summer school for the rest of the summer. Glad she didn't have to face him. Geez, the humiliation.

And she'd felt it again this morning, faced with Reverend John Peters on her front porch. And then with Missy.

Well, she was a big girl now. She had to brush it off and get over it.

And she would.

She'd voiced her feelings, and really didn't care to discuss them further. With Sam. With herself. But the biggest feeling she'd experienced in the past few minutes was relief. Suddenly, she knew Sam was telling her the truth. He didn't want Missy Hawkins.

He wanted her. Lucki.

He hadn't said it in so many words.

He didn't have to.

It was in his eyes. She saw it. He wanted her.

Maybe he even loved her.

Like she did him.

Chapter Eleven

"Lucki! Dammit! Get over here and quick! Where are the trophies? What did you do with the volleyballs? Who did you call to referee? No one has shown up yet! The tournament starts in ten minutes and we don't have a single thing ready! Rick is about to blow a gasket!"

Pinky grabbed Lucki no sooner than she had stepped out of Sam's car and herded her toward the tournament registration table. She glanced briefly back at Sam as he was exiting the driver's side, gave him a weak shrug, and then turned back to Pinky.

"The volleyballs are in Matt's truck, Pinky. We put them there yesterday. The trophies are safe, locked in the cab of my truck. We can get them later. Hank Snider is coming to referee, and he's bringing someone with him. He's always right on time, never early, never late. He'll be here, don't worry. And as far as Rick is concerned, cool it. He blows a gasket every other hour, you know that."

Lucki settled her gaze on Pinky and sighed. Geez, what would they ever do without her? Could no one around this joint function without her leadership?

Hey, maybe she was good for something after all, she chuckled to herself. Despite that she was a clumsy leg-breaker. Seems like neither Matt nor Pinky could take charge of anything without her direction. She should have been back here an hour ago.

"Just relax, Pinky, okay? Everything will be fine. Are the teams registered? Everyone get their shirts? Read the rules?"

"Yes, yes, and yes." Pinky shuffled through a stack of papers.

"Everyone has their time slots? Know when to show up here?"

Pinky nodded. "Yes and yes."

Lucki grinned. "See? You didn't need me after all, did you?"

Pinky's eyes grew wide. "Damned tootin' we need you! What if something goes wrong? What if...?"

Lucki laid a hand on her arm. "Pinky, relax. Everything is going to go just fine."

At that statement, she heard a shrill whistle. She glanced at her watch. Two o'clock. Time to begin. And Hank Snider had arrived, just like clockwork. Quickly, she gathered the first two teams together, made up of employees, their family members and friends, explained the rules one more time, appointed Hank referee omnipotent, the final authority, and let the games begin.

As the first volley was served, she glanced to her left and saw a smiling Sam watching her. A funny little tingle tripped up her spine, swirled around her neck, and caught in her throat.

Something dawned on her then. She liked him watching her with that saucy little grin on his face. Liked it a lot.

FOUR HOURS LATER, SAM STEPPED UP BEHIND LUCKI and grabbed her around the waist. She jumped and then turned in his arms, facing him.

"The tournament is over, Lucki. Let's go home."

And to bed.

Startled at the look in Lucki's eyes, he tightened his grip on her. Immobilizing her. "You in a hurry to get home?" she asked.

"Well, I don't want to leave J.J. and Spud together too long. You know the shenanigans they can get into."

"We should have brought him with us. Both of them. They would have had a ball."

Sam nodded. Yes, he should have. But with Missy's so-called emergency messing up his plans that morning, he'd opted for J.J. to stay at Spud's. "Couldn't be helped." Leaning closer, Sam touched the tip of his nose to Lucki's.

Immediately, she jumped back and pushed at his arms. "Sam. I'm working."

He released her.

"When are you finished?"

"About an hour," she replied.

"Then I can take you home?"

She hesitated. "Sam, I have my truck. I'll probably be late. You can head on home whenever you need to, all right? I'll probably come later, after we've gotten everything cleaned up."

Sam thought about that. He could stay and help Lucki, be next to her, wait for her. But perhaps he should go on. Fetch J.J. Feed the kid dinner. Get him settled for the night. And then wait for Lucki's return. Perhaps....

An enticing thought came to mind.

"It has been a long day, Lucki. I think I will go on home. Maybe I'll see you later?"

He knew the grin on his face was a sly one. Couldn't help it.

Lucki shuffled papers, rifled through a box of trophies, then shoved back a loose lock of hair and looked at him. She was tired. So, tired. Probably needed a hot bath. Bubble bath, maybe. And a massage. And something nice and relaxing to drink....

"Okay, Sam. I'll see you later."

She turned away, shouted something to Pinky, and then hoisted the box of leftover trophies to her hip. He gave her a small wave and turned to leave.

"Later, Lucki." But not too much later, my dear.

"Sam?"

He turned back. "Yes?"

"Thanks for being here this afternoon. Even if it didn't actually work out as planned. It was still nice having you here." She offered him a tired smile.

"No problem, Lucki." He grinned back.

No problem at all.

IT WAS MUCH LATER WHEN LUCKI GOT HOME. SO much so that she opted to skip an invitation for a late fast-food dinner with Pinky and Matt, and head on home. She was exhausted.

Smiling, she shook her head at the irony of the afternoon. Absolutely nothing had gone as planned. Reverend Peters had broken his leg. Missy had come to fetch him. Sam had smiled at her with that come-hither look on his face the entire day. And Pinky had made goo-goo eyes at Matt every chance she got. Thing was, he was doing the same thing back at her. It was nauseatingly sweet.

Secretly, Lucki was glad for the two of them. They both

needed someone. And she, herself, was glad to have Matt Farmer off her tail.

Exhausted, she pulled into her driveway, drove around back, and killed the car's engine. Silence. Blessed silence filled her ears. Perhaps she should just slink down in the seat and sleep here, she told herself. The thought was almost enticing, too tired to walk from the truck to her back door.

But she didn't. Dragging herself from the vehicle, she slowly made her way across the back yard, onto her back porch, into her kitchen, up the back stairway, down the hallway, and toward her bedroom without turning on a single light.

She blinked.

A soft murmur of light spilled from her bedroom door into the hallway. A soft, flickering of muted light. Somewhat radiant and sensual at the same time. Puzzled, she stepped inside.

A dozen or more lit candles graced her dresser, her bedside tables, and a bookshelf. Her bed was turned back, her pastel green sheets inviting in the dim light. A black lace negligee lay dark across the bed. On one bedside table sat an ice bucket holding a bottle of chilled champagne. Two fluted crystal glasses graced its left. A bowl of strawberries and another of chocolates to the right. Behind them all sat a dozen long-stemmed roses. By morning, they would be open and flowering, she knew.

By morning, she wondered if she'd be the same.

There was no doubt in her mind who had set up this scene of seduction. No doubt. And at the moment, she was too tired to fight it.

He stepped inside her bedroom then, and she turned to look at him. No words were spoken as Sam slowly came toward her, reaching out his hand. She lifted hers, their gazes connected, and he grasped her fingers and gently pulled her closer. Still without words, he led her out of the bedroom, down the hall, and into the bathroom.

More candles graced the large bathroom. The antique claw-foot tub, her mother's pride and joy, was full of bubbles and what she hoped, hot water. Fluffy towels stacked by its side. Incense burned and mingled with the scent of the candles.

Sam turned, stared longingly into her eyes, then reached to the bottom of her T-shirt and dragged it up and over her head. She let him.

Still, a little in awe of all this attention, but not questioning, she kept contact with his eyes. Slowly, gently, caressingly, he undressed her. Her silky bra, her denim shorts, her plain old cotton bikini panties, her Nikes, her athletic socks....

And then she stood before him. Naked. Shivering. Wanting him. Still watching his eyes. Still waiting.

Finally, his gaze played down over her body, perusing, sensually massaging. She shivered more intensely under his scrutiny as his eyes devoured her. Then he stepped closer, one-half step, and kissed her lips. Ever so lightly. Nibbling. Tasting. Their bodies still not touching. Only their lips.

Then he broke away and led her to the tub.

He motioned for her to step inside, and with a bashful glance his way, still holding onto his hand, she lifted first one foot and then the other into the tub's warmth. Within seconds, she slipped beneath the water and leaned back against the rear of the tub. A sigh escaped her lips unwillingly. Then Sam was there, a folded towel in hand, urging her to lay her head back.

She looked up at him.

"Relax, Lucki," he whispered. "Just relax. I'll take care of everything." He stroked several loose locks of hair from her forehead, then reaching back, undid the elastic holding her ponytail and let her hair fall free.

Lucki searched his face, and her breath caught in her throat. That he would go to this length to please her, to woo her... What did it mean? Was Sam, the boy-next-door, *really* in love with her? Was this forever?

Or was she just another conquest?

Another woman to coo and woo and wine and dine?

God, she hoped not. Because after this night, she knew there would be no turning back. For the first time in her life, she felt like being swept away. Transcended. Blissfully held and pampered and made love to. And when all this was through, she knew, beyond any doubt, she would be in love with Sam Kirk for the rest of her life.

And probably always had been.

The only question—would he remain in love with her?

Was this a risk she was willing to take?

And as she eased her head back against the tub, sliding deeper into the sensuous warmth of water and bubbles and Sam's gaze, she knew she would take that chance.

She closed her eyes.

A ripple bounced against her chest, and she opened them again briefly. Sam had dipped a washcloth in the water and was wringing out the excess. Settling down beside her outside the tub, he stroked the warm cloth over her face, and Lucki closed her eyes again. She felt the tiny nubs of the cloth scrape slightly over her skin, behind her ear, around her neck, and down over her collarbone.

Relaxed, so relaxed, Lucki felt herself falling into a dizzying state of another world as her senses took over and her tired body surrendered to Sam's caresses.

She slid deeper into the water.

Within seconds, it seemed, the water sloshed again, only with more intensity, and she opened her eyes to see a now naked Sam stepping inside the tub with her.

"May I?" he whispered.

"Of course." *Why is my voice all raspy?*

"Sit up and turn around. Okay?" She did. Sam eased into a sitting position behind her, the water sluicing up slightly over the side. Then he pulled her back down against his chest and wrapped his arms around her.

"Umm...." he purred in her ear. "Finally."

Lucki turned and settled her cheek into the crook of his neck and shoulder. Sam tightened his embrace. He wrapped his legs around hers, holding her close. Lucki fell into a complete state of bliss.

Candles flickered. Incense burned. Bubbles caressed.

Sam's hands and fingers and arms and legs aligned with hers. Bliss. Pure bliss. There was no other way to describe it. She felt herself being lulled into a near state of sleepiness.

"Tired, honey?"

Lucki nodded into his shoulder. When had Sam Kirk felt so good? Became such a tender and sweet lover?

His hands started their search then, gently, slowly caressing over her chest, her breasts. He gently pinched her nipples, rolling them between his thumb and forefinger. Currents of desire spread warm throughout her body. The pads of his fingers grazed the sides of her breasts and she exhaled. He spanned her waist with his hands, dipped lower past her navel, and then finally slid one between her legs.

Lucki shivered with mounting heat.

Heat that wasn't coming from the bath.

He gently caressed her with his fingertips, holding her there, slowly increasing the pressure. Never urgent, just lazy, swirling touches. Lucki didn't know when touching had felt so good. He rubbed his leg along hers. Gentle splashes of water swept over the side of the tub.

She didn't care. She was being held. Caressed. By Sam. Nothing else at this moment mattered. Nothing else.

After a while, Sam pushed her forward, away from his chest. "Lean up, honey. Let me wash your hair."

Reluctantly, not wanting to leave his warmth, Lucki did. She sat up, letting her hair fall back as Sam dipped water over her hair and let it fall in a cascade over him. Next, he lathered shampoo in his hands, tangled his fingers in her hair, and massaged the creamy lotion into her scalp.

Lucki nearly had to lean back against him again. His fingers on her head, in her hair, felt so good, so relaxing, and very sensual. The pads of his fingertips massaged as he worked the lather through her hair. Never had she felt so pampered, so loved.

Never had she suspected Sam could be so giving.

He took his time, threading his fingers through her hair, gently massaging. Lucki closed her eyes. His hands and magic fingers slowly drifted from her scalp down to her neck, where he gently kneaded her tired muscles. Then to her shoulders. She felt her head lulling to one side as his soap-covered fingers worked their way down the knotted kinks in her back.

"Didn't realize you were so tied up in knots," he whispered as every aching cord, every hard lump of muscle became like putty in his hands.

"I didn't either," she whispered back. "Sam, that feels so good."

He leaned closer. "And we've only just started, honey."

His breath was warm against her ear.

She shivered.

What seemed seconds later, Sam had rinsed her hair and body and had stepped out of the tub. He held her hand as she stepped out and then drew a large terry towel around the two of them.

Their bodies meshed in warmth and wetness, he nestled her into a cocoon intended only for themselves. She could feel his heart beating against her cheek. She could feel the powerful heat of his groin, the weight of his sex against her belly. And she nuzzled closer into him as he once again took control and toweled her hair.

Then, easing slightly away, they took turns toweling each other dry, never breaking eye contact. Not once.

A strange feeling washed over Lucki. Familiar. Desirable. And then again, so foreign. So new.

She wanted to feel this over and over and over again.

With Sam.

Every time they made love.

For the rest of their lives.

God, she was hopelessly in love with him.

In the bedroom, the muted flickering light cast a sort of medieval ambiance about the room. Sam stepped to the bed, picked up the black negligee, and returned to her. He placed it over her head and slowly drew it down over her body. When finished, he stood back. Admiring her.

It felt so unusual to be the object of such doting.

"You are so beautiful, Lucki."

His eyes met hers, and she watched him smile.

"I love you," he whispered. "You know that, don't you? And I wanted you to know that before things went any further."

She dipped her head in a nod, suddenly feeling very shy and naïve. "Yes, I know that."

"You are so sexy."

Glancing quickly down at herself, Lucki shrugged. "Just a nightgown...."

He stepped forward then, grasped her hand, and turned her toward her dresser mirror. Standing behind her, he reached around and clasped his hands about her waist. "Look at you, Lucki. You're beautiful. Sexy. And mine."

Something indescribable tripped through her then at lightning speed. She looked. And watched. And she could only feel as if Sam's hands moved along the curves and contours of her body. Along her hips. Up the sides to her breasts. Cupping them. And then down again to her belly, cupping her bottom, and then her aching mound. She wanted his touch. Wanted him.

His eyes met hers in the mirror.

The negligee was gone, suddenly whipped away. His hands were on her flesh, touching her as before. She felt more aroused than she'd ever felt in her entire life. Watching him touch her in the mirror was nearly her undoing.

Turning, she drew him in, and placed her hands on either side of his face. Kissing him, like she'd never kissed him before, she could only think of how wonderful his kisses were going to be for the rest of her life. Waking with kisses like this. Going to bed with kisses like this. Stealing kisses like this throughout every day.

How could a girl get so lucky?

"Lucki, the bed," Sam croaked. And before he could say it twice, they were there.

He covered her. Rained kisses over her. And she let him take his fill. She explored. As did he. And within seconds, Lucki let him in, knowing that at last, she had found her love. He rocked her. Right to her very center. And she loved being filled with him.

When she exploded around him, and he shuddered in release, she knew it was only the beginning for them. All this time. All the years they'd known each other.

It was only the beginning.

And it was. Just the beginning of a long, wonderful night. Sleep eluded them for most of it, and they never got to the champagne and strawberries.

Chapter Twelve

"Lucki!"

Someone shouted at her. From the far end of an endless tunnel. The voice was familiar, yes, but she couldn't quite distinguish....

"*Lucki!*"

Groggily, she turned over. Felt something stop her. And had to think about that a minute. Something was in her bed. Something large, hard, warm, and male.

"Lucki! I know you're in there! Your truck is outside!"

Footsteps started down the upstairs hallway and toward her bedroom.

"Have you seen Sam? He's not at home."

Sam? *Sam?*

Lucki opened her eyes. Looked to her left. There he was. Sam. Zonked out beside her, his arms wrapped around one of her pillows, his mouth a little droopy, a soft snore filtering from his nose. Damn.

Sam. In her bed.

Oh, so cute when he sleeps!

God, they'd practically worn each other out all night.

Reality hit her.

The footsteps stopped outside the door.

She bounded up, taking a blanket with her. "J.J.? Don't come in! I'm getting dressed!"

"You're late, you know that?"

Damnation! Lucki's gaze swept the room. *Damnation!* She looked at her sleeping Sam. Oh, God! J.J. couldn't find him here like this!

Late? *Late?*

"Have you seen Sam, Lucki?" he called through the door.

Yes, she'd seen him. All of him.

"Hold on, J.J., I'll be right out."

"Well, he was supposed to have picked me up from Spud's early this morning so I could go with you to the park. It's after nine. I guess he forgot and went on to the office. Spud's mom dropped me off. You going into work today?"

Lucki stopped mid-motion. Work?

She glanced at the clock. Nine-thirty-two. *Hell's bells. It's Wednesday!* She was supposed to be at work at eight!

"Yes! Hold on...."

Racing across the room, she grabbed panties...bra...T-shirt...shorts...socks...shoes.... And put on what she could.

Sam. Damn. She had to wake him.

The phone rang.

Oh, shit.

J.J. pounded on the door. "Lucki are you coming? 'Cause if you aren't, me and Spud...."

"Hold *on* J.J!"

She picked up the phone. "Hello?"

"Lucki? Kathleen here. Have you seen Sam this morning? He's late for his nine-o'clock appointment. Hasn't called in. Won't answer his phone. I'm a little worried. Unlike him. Can you go check?"

Double Damn. Kathleen, the town gossip. Now the whole world will know. Have to handle this carefully.

"Kathleen. I'll try. Call you back. Okay?" Suddenly, she was out of breath.

"Lucki, you okay?"

"Yes."

"You're sure?"

"Yes. Just in a hurry. Late for work. I'll call back."

"Okay honey. Just worried about him."

"Don't. He's okay. He'll call in a bit, I'm sure."

She hung up the phone.

Sheesh....

She turned to Sam.

J.J. knocked on the door again. "Lucki? What are you *doing* in there? Are you going to work or not 'cause Spud and me...."

Lucki kneeled on the bed and stroked Sam's cheek. "In a minute!" She leaned closer and whispered into his ear. "Sam. Sam, darling, you have to get up."

He mumbled something.

"Sam. You have to go to work."

He turned over and mumbled something else.

"Sam." She said it louder this time and shook him.

He snorted.

"Sam. You have to get up!" She was getting impatient. "Kathleen called. J.J.'s outside my bedroom door. And I have to go to work. So do you. Sam. Wake up, dammit!" Frustration bit at her.

He roused.

Looked at her.

Then smiling, reached up and pulled her down on top of him.

She let him. Couldn't help it.

His kisses, so familiar now, still took her by surprise, and melted her insides. His lips, soft, caressing, just about turned her into melted gelatin. She loved kissing him. Could kiss him all day. If only they didn't have to go to work....

He flipped her then, rolling over on top of her, groaning. She groaned right along with him.

Finally, he broke the kiss, looked into her eyes, and ran his fingers through the hair at her temples. "Good morning, lover," he said in the most sexy voice.

"Good morning to you," Lucki croaked.

He smiled, and gazed into her eyes.

Lucki smiled back.

"You're dressed."

"I know."

"I like you better naked."

"I'd rather be naked."

"Then why are you dressed?"

"Because...."

J.J. pounded on the door again. "Darn it, Lucki! What's going on in there?"

Then the phone rang again.

Sam's eyes grew large.

"I have to get that."

"What the hell is going on here?" Sam glanced at the door and sat up.

"Three ring circus. Feel lucky you've slept through part of it." She grinned and reached for the phone.

Then came pounding from downstairs.

"Lucki, someone's at your door downstairs," J.J. called out.

Lucki lifted the phone to her ear and rolled her eyes at Sam. "Hello?"

Pinky blasted some incoherent sentences into her ear.

"Lucki! Want me to get that door downstairs?"

She lowered the phone. Sam started to reply to his brother.

She stopped him with a hand over his mouth and a shake of her head. "Yes, J.J., please do that, okay?"

Sam gave her a puzzled look.

She returned to a still-ranting Pinky.

"Pinky, slow down. What's wrong?"

"Where in the hell are you? We had a board meeting this morning!"

Oh hell! "Overslept, Pink. I'm on my way. Thirty minutes. Did Rick go ballistic?"

"Rick always goes ballistic. Get your tail in here. Pronto. That's not the half of it." Geez. When it rains...."

"I'm leaving now."

She replaced the receiver. Got up off the bed. Glanced nervously at Sam.

"What the hell is going on here?"

Lucki sat down on the floor to finish putting on her Nikes. She glanced back up at him. "Okay, in a nutshell. It's Wednesday. Both of us are supposed to be at work. J.J. came looking for you when you didn't pick him up at Spud's this morning. Kathleen called, you missed your nine o'clock. That was Pinky on the phone. I missed a board meeting and Rick is furious. You need to get out of here before J.J. gets back upstairs. And I have no idea who is at the front door."

He stared at her.

"C'mon, Sam. Get up! Get dressed! And get home before J.J. gets back up here."

"Why do you want me out of here so quickly? I can leave after you leave with J.J."

She thought about that. "Maybe you should be home when J.J. goes back there, so he knows you are okay."

"You just don't want people to know we slept together last night, do you?"

His words stunned her. She blinked. Did she?

She did.

He was right. Not that she would admit that to him. She had barely admitted it to herself.

But she lied by saying, "That's ridiculous. I don't think a twelve-year-old child needs to see his brother in his next-door neighbor's bed."

He pondered that. "All right. I'll agree with you there."

She breathed a silent sigh of relief.

"So get dressed okay?"

He nodded. "Okay."

He took his old good time about it.

Long enough for her to ponder his statement. Hells bells. She *didn't* want anyone to know they'd slept together last night. The whole town would know in a flash, and then everyone would consider them a couple, and wasn't that really what she wanted? Was it?

What did she want? Sam?

Did it matter that everyone in Harbor Falls knew that they had made love?

Yes, of course it did. Because she knew this small town. And from the get-go they would start making plans.

Plans.

All sorts of plans.

For the two of them. The busybodies would have a heyday. Two of Harbor Falls own. Childhood friends. Oh, what they would do with this at church.

Oh, God. Did she *want* that?

Because, if all of Harbor Falls knew about them, then they would be an item.

And if they were an item, then everyone would assume they would get engaged.

And if they were engaged, then they would eventually get married.

And then....

But—

If Sam, *The Heartbreaker*, decided that all the plans were too confining, too much for him to handle, too constricting, and then decided to break *her* heart, then all of Harbor Falls would know that, too. And she would be the laughingstock. Or maybe, just the object of their pity for way too long.

She'd seen it happen with others. When Shelley Hart ran off with her sister's fiancé, poor Suzie Hart suffered from the towns-folks pity for months on end.

But it eventually turned out all right for Suzie, didn't it?

Still, she had to keep this quiet for a while. Had to. Just for a while. Until she was certain. Until she knew that Sam was totally devoted. That he would not break her heart. That he loved her unconditionally, wanted to be her lifelong partner and had mended all his heartbreaking ways for good.

She had to be sure that Sam wanted forever. Because *she* wanted forever.

Yes, she did.

With Sam now dressed, she turned to him and gave him a quick peck on the lips. "See you later?" she whispered. Her hand rested on the doorknob. Her heart thrummed despite herself.

She couldn't help it. She loved him.

He pulled her close and wrapped his arms around her. "That little peck won't do, Lucki." He grinned and kissed her then. Fully. Passionately. Deeply. His mouth raking over hers. His tongue playing with hers. Wet. Sloppy. Juicy. And long.

Her hand slipped off the doorknob, and she put her arms around his neck to pull him even closer.

She deepened the kiss.

The door creaked open. She didn't care.

They finished their kiss.

Then turned toward the hallway.

J.J. and Kathleen stood there, mouths agape, watching the entire kiss, she supposed, in surprised and utter silence.

Damn. Double damn.

Sᴀᴍ ᴡʜɪsᴛʟᴇᴅ ᴀs ʜᴇ sᴛᴇᴘᴘᴇᴅ ɪɴᴛᴏ ʜɪs ᴏꜰꜰɪᴄᴇ ᴀɴᴅ slapped down the last patient folder of the day. And it was a long day. He'd avoided the silent smirking, the knowing evil little grins Kathleen had tossed him the rest of the morning and the entire afternoon.

He hadn't spoken a word to her about the morning's incident. Not even at Lucki's house.

Instead, he had excused himself with only a nod to Kathleen, a brotherly look to J.J., and a wink to Lucki. He watched Lucki's eyes widen in embarrassment as he started down the hallway. He felt a little guilty leaving her to the explanations, but figured she could handle it. No one thought on her feet better than Lucki.

Before long, he was back at his house, showering, and getting ready to leave for the office. He managed to avoid J.J. as his younger brother called goodbye to him through the shower curtain. He'd opted for a day of fishing with Spud instead of heading to Harbor Falls with Lucki. He figured that was probably best; he knew Lucki had her own dilemma to handle at work.

His patients would just have to understand. Sometimes, physicians have emergencies. And last night was definitely an emergency. He'd needed Lucki badly. He just might have exploded had he not made love to her when he did.

And Lucki, damn, he'd did not know how wonderful a lover she could be. Attentive. Daring. Wanting him.

He wanted her. Forever. There was absolutely no doubt in his mind. First chance he got, he was going to explain that to her. Thoroughly. Right after he loved her until she was too weak to protest or give him any lip about it. Then, once he had her commitment, there was no way he would ever let her back out of it.

Lucki Stevenson, the girl next door, was going to be his woman. His wife. And nothing, absolutely nothing in this world, could make him any more ecstatic. Nothing.

He'd finally realized what had been under his nose all along.

He loved Lucki.

Always had. Always will.

And that's why none of the other women could ever keep his interest for long. None of the other women could ever compare to Lucki. His Lucki.

Why had it taken him so long to realize that?

"Still whistling, Doctor?"

Kathleen leaned against his doorjamb, her arms crossed over her over-large midriff.

"Whistling? Me?"

Sam grinned and returned to his desk. What the hell if Kathleen knew? She'd been a good friend the past few months, helping him get his practice up and going, running an efficient office.

"So, it looks like love on that face to me, Dr. Kirk."

"It does, Kathleen? Tell me, what does love look like?"

"Just look in the mirror, Doctor. Or look at Lucki's face the next time you see her. When did all this happen, if I might ask?"

Sam glanced away from Kathleen and thought about that. When had all this come about? Thing was, he couldn't exactly pinpoint it. He guessed it just had always been.

"Hard to say there, Kathleen. Hard to say."

"So when do we hear wedding bells?" She grinned and winked at him.

"Wedding bells?"

"Yes. Wedding bells, Sam. I'm sure that's been on your

mind, hasn't it? I mean, all these years, we've all been waiting for you two to realize what we've known all along. You two were meant for each other. Now, when can I plan a wedding shower?"

"Wedding shower?"

Suddenly, Sam wasn't sure Kathleen knowing this was a good idea. Lucki, he knew, would go berserk if she heard Kathleen talk like this. It was too new. Too fragile right now. He'd only had one night with her. And it had taken him forever to convince her that they belonged together. It had taken some planning to set the seduction scene the night before.

No, Kathleen had to back off. He had to stop her. Now. Before she ruined everything.

Before Lucki got wind of this, and turned tail and ran.

"Look Kathleen. No wedding bells, okay? We're not planning anything..." *Yet.* "No showers either. The timing isn't right. Lucki and I have no plans." *Yet.* "Lucki and I—well, yes, we do share something a little more intimate than most friends." *That's an understatement.* "But there will be no wedding bells." *Yet.* "So please don't make any plans, okay?"

He really wasn't good at lying under his breath.

"But you are getting married, right?"

Damn. She could ruin everything if she took this and ran with it.

"No, Kathleen. Lucki and I have no plans for marriage." *Not yet, at least.* "But if we do, I promise you, Kathleen, you will be the first to know to spread the word."

Sam crossed his fingers behind his back. He hoped Kathleen would cool off, forget this conversation, and let everything die down for a while. He needed more time with Lucki. Lots more time to convince her she was meant for him, that he was meant for her. That he would love her until the end of time. That they would be a wonderful team together. And that someday, they would be excellent parents together.

Suddenly, the thought of him and Lucki being parents made him feel extremely satisfied. Was this what he'd been looking for all his adult life? Memphis had never satisfied him. The practice there was lucrative, however a bit stifling. Here, in Harbor Falls, he'd felt so much more at home. Much more relaxed. Suddenly, he realized that he needed Lucki to complete that picture. He needed Lucki in his life, in his bed, and needed her bringing his children into the world, to make both their lives worth living.

All is right with the world, he thought.

All is definitely right with the world.

Chapter Thirteen

"And I expect you to be at board meetings," Rick added.

"Yes, sir." She nodded. Why did she suddenly feel so small and insignificant sitting across from Rick's desk?

"We were discussing the new skateboard park, and you were the only one who had all the statistics and figures on that. It was your baby, Lucki. The kids are going to be disappointed."

She swallowed. Hard. She'd let down her kids.

"Can we call a special meeting? Isn't there anything I can do?"

Rick shook his head. "Board members are extremely busy people. You know that. Most have their own businesses to run. We're lucky if we get them here for quarterly meetings. This is a project they were interested in. They want to see these kids off the streets, off their sidewalks, away from their business doors, and someplace safe. It's not that they don't want them there because they think it will hurt their businesses. They want them off the street for safety reasons."

"I understand that, Rick." She pondered the situation for

a minute. "What if I go to each board member separately? Granted, it will take a little more time, but I'll do it on my time, after work. Perhaps if I give them a one-on-one presentation, it will be more personal anyway. Perhaps not cost-effective, but more personal."

He stared at her and then rubbed his chin. "It's a thought, Lucki. We have to get the advisory board behind us before we go to the city and county councils to ask for more money. We need our ducks in a row. I want to be at the city council meeting in one week, the county meets shortly after that. If we want to start construction on this thing early spring, we have to get moving now. We have to get our funding sources lined up and assure the community that this is a good thing. Oh, and I need the information on that grant you were looking into. The more outside money we can snag, the better, I think."

Lucki stood. "I agree, Rick. I'll get right on it."

"Do that, Lucki."

He nodded, and she nodded back.

After leaving his office, she breathed a deep sigh of relief. She'd screwed up. But she had a chance at retribution. She could do this. She could make the board see the positive side of this, then she could take it to the local government. *I can do this.*

And she would.

"Everything okay in there, Lucki?"

She turned toward Pinky's voice. Somehow, she looked different.

"I smoothed it over. Have my work cut out for me though."

"The skateboard park?"

"Yeah."

She stared at Pinky again. "Pinky, what have you done with yourself that's different?"

Pinky grinned ear to ear. "Died my hair back to its natural shade. I like it better this way."

"That's it! So do I, Pink. It looks great!"

"Matt likes it better this way, too."

"You did this last night? Yesterday, it was blonde."

"Well, yes. Matt commented he liked it the old way better, so I thought I'd surprise him this morning."

"And...?"

Pinky grinned again, widely. "He loved it."

Lucki smiled at her friend. "Pinky, I couldn't be more pleased." And she meant that, sincerely.

Seemed like everyone was falling in love these days.

AS SOON AS SHE STEPPED INSIDE HER KITCHEN DOOR, her phone shattered the silence. Goodness! Did that thing ever stop ringing?

"Hello?"

"Hi lover."

Lucki melted. She loved hearing Sam call her that.

"Hi, Sam." She was blushing for sure. Her cheeks were hot.

"Was waiting for you to get home. How was your day?"

Lucki exhaled. "Long. Tiring. Complex."

"Too tired for dinner out?"

Closing her eyes, Lucki leaned against the kitchen counter. "Out?"

"Yes. How about dinner at *a la Lucie's* in a couple of hours?"

"A couple of hours?"

"You need more time to get ready?"

"More like a little time to unwind a bit."

"I understand that. It's early honey. How about if I come

over about seven, we get to the restaurant about eight, have a late dinner and then come back here?"

"We both have to work tomorrow, Sam."

"I know. We can swing it. We're young."

She needed some downtime. And she wanted to see him. Dinner at *a la Lucie's* would be absolute heaven. It had been ages since she'd eaten anywhere that didn't have paper napkins and straws.

"Why don't you come over here around six-thirty? We'll get a little earlier start then."

She could almost sense Sam grinning through the phone.

"Sure thing, lover."

A chill ran through her. "Bye, Sam. See you in a while."

"Can't wait." She thought she heard a kiss through the phone.

It took her only a few minutes to run a nice, warm bath, assess her closet for the right outfit, and slip into the tub for an hour of unwinding. She could get used to this.

She could get used to coming home every day to Sam Kirk and his surprises. *Yes sir.* She sure could.

THE RESTAURANT, *A LA LUCIE'S,* HELD EVERY BIT OF romantic ambiance a woman could want, Lucki decided, as she stepped into the restaurant on Sam's arm. It had been ages since she'd been there. Not since her parents had taken her out to celebrate her twenty-first birthday. She'd never been here with a man, so this was a special treat for her. That Sam would bring her here was even more special.

He turned and grinned, and Lucki had to shake herself at the newness of all this. Sam, her best friend since childhood, now her lover. It was a concept her brain was having little trouble dealing with. It seemed right. Like it should have been this way all along. Yet, foreign and a little odd.

Knowing Sam so intimately was going to take a little getting used to.

But a task she was not averse to. In fact, it was a task she quite welcomed.

They were seated across from each other at a small table in a darkened corner of the Italian restaurant. A candle flickered from the center. A single rose in a crystal bud vase graced the table. The restaurant smelled of Italian spices and tomatoes and scented candles. Low conversation fluttered across the room. An old-world charm enveloped them. The server arrived, providing menus and glasses of water with lemon, and then they were alone.

Sam reached across the table and took her hand. "Lucinda Stevenson, you are so very beautiful."

Immediately, she blushed. "It's because of you," she whispered.

"No, you've always been beautiful, Lucki. It's just now I know you are *my* beautiful woman."

Lucki's gaze played with his. "Am I Sam?" she returned softly. "Am I yours?"

"Always, honey."

"Always?" *As in forever?*

Their server came then and interrupted the moment. Sam ordered the veal. Lucki opted for bowtie pasta and vegetables. Each requested a salad, dressing on the side. Sam ordered a red wine. Finally, the server left.

"You were saying?" Lucki hinted. She had to know where Sam was coming from.

He leaned closer, drawing her hand further into his. "Lucki. Don't you know? Can't you feel it?"

Yes, she could feel it. But she had to know it. What were Sam's intentions here? "Tell me, Sam."

"I love you," he whispered, a heart-felt look upon his face. "Don't you know that yet?"

She nodded. She knew it. But was it a lasting kind of love? "I love you, too, Sam, but—"

He gripped her hand tighter. "There are no buts here, Lucki. We love each other. From there we can build—"

"Your wine, sir."

The server placed two glasses of the red before them. Sam nodded to the server who quickly left. Then he tipped his glass toward Lucki. "Toast?"

She nodded and lifted her glass.

"To us."

"To us," she repeated, sort of hanging in a spellbound mist. Was this happening? Did he truly and forever love her? Then she touched her glass to his. They both took a sip of the warm wine.

Sam held his glass in the air a moment longer, pausing. "To a lifetime together."

He tipped his glass forward again. Lucki hesitated.

"Lucki?"

Searching his face, Lucki finally let go of her anxieties. A lifetime. His words. He wanted a lifetime together. With her.

"To a lifetime together, Sam. Our lifetime."

She touched her glass to his once more, and then both sipped the wine as they held each other's gaze. When Sam at last sat his glass on the table, he leaned closer and drew her closer.

"Lucki, will you marry me?"

She felt like clutching her heart. She was sure it was going to jump out of her chest. Marry him? Marry Sam?

Was this it? Was he actually, finally, totally willing to commit to one woman? And was that one woman *her*?

She studied his face for a moment and knew that this man, this grown-up, boy-next-door, was the only man she'd ever wanted to share her life. Ever. He'd always been the only man for her.

"Yes, Sam. I will. I will marry you," she whispered, and breathed a sigh of relief. It was official, and she didn't care who the hell in Harbor Falls knew it!

Lucki wasn't sure which of them exhaled the hardest.

"Oh, thank God." Sam whooshed out another breath. "I don't have a ring yet but—"

She didn't care. Leaning over the table, she grasped Sam by his jacket lapels, yanked him closer, and kissed him square on the lips.

It was a kiss *a la Lucie's* would not soon forget.

ALL DAY THURSDAY, LUCKI WORKED ON THE skateboard project. It was late when she finally got home. She'd holed herself up in her cubicle and dared anyone to open her door. She researched grant possibilities. Made appointments with board members. She even lined up a couple of young skateboarders to come with her so the business community could see for themselves that these kids were not just juvenile delinquent punks. By the end of the day, she was pleased with her progress.

Friday put her on the road, seeing through her appointments. It was a long day but a fruitful one. Every single board member agreed with her suggestions. Every single board member stated their support of the project. And every single board member was impressed by the articulate young skateboarders she'd brought with her. So much so that the board felt it was a good idea to bring along the young men to the council meetings. Lucki agreed. Her plan was working. By spring, the skateboard park could be a reality.

Through all this, she and Sam had had limited time

together. Even though they'd not had time to actually "date," Sam had managed to sneak up Lucki's back staircase for a few hours of intimacy each night. Lucki waited for him, knowing he would be there, and looked forward to the day when they wouldn't have to sneak anymore.

Saturday morning, she slept in. How long had it been since she'd done that? But at ten minutes after ten, her phone rang, interrupting her silence.

"'Morning, love."

Sam. Ah, so nice to hear his voice. Hadn't he just left hours before? "Hi, baby." She liked calling him that. Called him that a lot lately.

"You up yet?"

"Just waking. You?"

"Umm...same here. Plans for the day?"

"Not really."

"I was just thinking. Maybe we should go see Reverend Peters."

In mid-stretch, Lucki's ears perked up. "Reverend Peters?"

Sam chuckled on the other end. She knew that chuckle. He had something on his mind.

"I mean, it's been a few days. Have you seen him since he broke his leg? I was just wondering how he was doing."

"Omigosh! I've been so busy, so distracted, I forgot all about that! Yes, Sam, I think we should go see him."

"That's what I thought, too. I'll be over in an hour. That okay?"

"Sure. Fine."

Lucki hung up the phone and stretched again. Staring at her ceiling, she contemplated their conversation. Thought about it for a while. There was just something.... Something not quite right.

Then it dawned on her.

"Sam Kirk, you sly devil," she said aloud. "You don't want

to see Reverend Peters about his broken leg. You want to see him about us getting married. You don't fool me, you bad boy you."

At that, Lucki grinned, ecstatically hopped out of her bed, and rushed for the shower. She and Sam were going to the preacher.

Life was good.

———

THE PARSONAGE SAT NEXT TO THE CHURCH, BUT when they knocked on the door, there was no answer. They wondered if Reverend Peters was well enough to venture to his office at the church and headed that way.

"The break must not have been too bad then," Lucki tried to reassure herself.

"I'm sure he's able to get around on crutches all right," Sam replied.

He held her hand as they stepped into the vestibule and then walked down the stairway into the church basement. "I'm sure he's fine, Lucki, and doesn't harbor any ill feelings toward you."

Lucki hoped not. But as concerned as she was for the good Reverend, she was trying to tamp down the butterflies in her tummy right now. She had other things on her mind besides Reverend Peters' broken leg. She knew Sam had other things on his mind, too. He kept looking at her and winking every chance he got. He definitely had other things on his mind. Not fooling her. Not in the least. She knew exactly what they were going to discuss with Reverend Peters.

Their wedding.

The thought made Lucki tingle. She almost wanted to giggle. Giddily giggle. And she was not the giggling type. Guess that's what falling in love does to you. Wonder how long Sam wanted to wait? Would he want a quick wedding? A big one with all the trimmings? A small, intimate one? What did she want? They had lots to discuss.

Oh gosh. She had to get in touch with her parents! Where would they be now? Somewhere in Colorado, she suspected. She would call her mom as soon as she and Sam were back home.

They neared the church office. The door stood partially ajar.

"I guess he's here." Lucki pointed toward the door.

Sam looked down and grinned. "Good." He squeezed her hand. Before he stepped closer to the door, however, he leaned over and placed a nice little kiss on her lips. Lucki fleetingly recalled the last time she'd kissed Sam in church. In the choir loft. In front of the entire congregation.

Next time we kiss in church, Sam Kirk, I expect it to be at our wedding.

She wished she would have said that out loud, but she didn't want to spoil his surprise. Perhaps, no, he wouldn't have done that, would he? Well, yes, maybe he would have. Would he have a ring for her today? That would be perfect. They she could finally tell the world. That it was all official. That they were an item. A couple. A pair.

It was happening. She and Sam were getting married.

Just as Sam lifted his fist to the office door, voices filtered out from a Sunday School classroom to their left. Sam stilled his knock.

Lucki turned toward the voices.

"The Methodist Women must be meeting," Sam suggested.

Lucki nodded.

Sam lifted his hand again.

"Wait." Lucki strained to hear... Had she heard her name? "What?"

"Sh... Just a second."

Then another voice, a familiar and loud voice, interjected the soft mumblings. "Well, I think we're all getting worked up about nothing if you ask me." It was Missy Hawkins.

Lucki looked at Sam. He mouthed the word, *Missy?*

She nodded. Another voice continued. "But we have to make plans, you all. We can't let this go by. I think a surprise shower is the best thing we can do."

Lucki shrugged. "Sounds like they are planning a shower for someone. Wonder who's having a baby?" Guess she hadn't heard her name after all.

Sam shook his head. "Haven't a clue." He turned back to the office door and lifted his fist.

Missy's voice peeled out. "Well, I for one, do not think Sam Kirk and Lucki Stevenson are going to get married. I think we're wasting our time planning some shower for a wedding that will never take place."

Lucki stilled and grasped Sam's arm. What in the world?

"Well, Missy Hawkins? What makes you such an authority on the subject, huh? We thought you were over Sam. You and the Reverend have seen quite a bit of each other lately. That has not gone unnoticed by most of Harbor Falls."

"Yes, Missy," another voice chimed in, "We know they are dating. Kathleen Conner has given us almost daily reports. Sam told her he was in love with Lucki. And have you seen her? She looks like she's on cloud nine."

"And it was reported," another woman added," that they shared a very intimate dinner at *a la Lucie's* the other night. Said Lucki kissed Sam right there in the middle of the restaurant. Seemed they were celebrating something. Or so I was told."

"And then, of course, there was that kiss last Sunday at church. My. What a barn burner!"

"Louise! You shouldn't be thinking such thoughts. You're seventy-five years old!"

Louise snickered. "But I'm not dead, Hannah. Not by a longshot."

"Well, this is all beside the point. Sam and Lucki are *not* getting married. I know that for a fact!" Missy shouted her final two cents worth.

Lucki turned to Sam. "What is this all about?" She was trying not to panic.

He shook his head. "I have no idea. Just some old women gathering wool." He pulled her toward the office. "Now, let's go see—"

She put up a hand. "Wait a minute."

The voice on the other side of the way continued, "And please tell us, Missy, how you know this?"

Missy continued. "Because Kathleen told me. She said she asked Sam point-blank if he and Lucki were getting married. She said he told her an emphatic *no*. That he and Lucki were good friends. Intimate friends, which to me means they are sleeping together, but that they have no plans to get married. None whatsoever. Kathleen said he told her, most definitely, that he and Lucki were *not* making wedding plans." She paused, for effect, likely.

"If you don't believe me, ask Kathleen yourself. In fact, I can call her."

Lucki stared straight ahead.

She felt numb.

So, Sam had told Kathleen they were intimate friends with no plans for marriage?

No plans for marriage?

God, he'd made a fool out of her again.

She turned to Sam. "Is that true?"

Sam licked his lips. "Is what true?"

"Did you say those things to Kathleen?"

Sam hesitated.

"Did you?"

He nodded. "Yes, but—"

She slapped him then, and the sound reverberated through the cavernous basement.

As she hurriedly climbed the stairs, away from Sam and the gossipmongers, she heard the scurry of chairs and the shuffle of feet from the Sunday School room next door. Then Sam called out to her.

She didn't answer. She'd be damned if she'd stick around for the humiliation and embarrassment of being the latest heartbreak victim of Dr. Sam Kirk.

DAZED, SAM WATCHED LUCKI FLEE UP THE STEPS. *What in the hell just happened here?*

"Looks like she overheard us. Sorry, Sam. We didn't know you two were out here."

Sam turned. The entire membership of the Harbor Falls Methodist Women stood before him, minus Kathleen Conner. Reverend Peters hobbled from his office as well.

"Did someone get slapped out here?" he asked.

Every eye in the room went to Sam's face then, and he lifted a hand to his hot cheek.

"You've got a nice handprint there, Sammy boy," Eloise Hunter offered. "Now what got into Lucki?"

"I think I have a pretty good idea."

He knew exactly what had gotten into Lucki. They were coming to Reverend Peters to talk about getting married. And then....

He scanned the room. All eyes were still on him. "Lucki had her heart broken. And each one of you is to blame. And each one of you is going to get me out of this situation. Do you hear me?"

Reverend Peters, Missy Hawkins, Eloise Hunter, and every other woman and the room bounced glances off each other. One by one, he felt the situation was dawning on them.

"Let's get this straight right now. I am *in love* with Lucki Stevenson. I want to marry her. I've even asked her, and she said yes. But she doesn't trust me, not yet. Overhearing that conversation sure must have been a blow to her. I was finally getting her to realize that I wanted to spend the rest of my life with her. And now...."

"Now, we've blown it for you, right, Sam?" For once, Missy looked almost apologetic.

"Yes, Missy. You all sure blew it."

"And now you need our help?" Reverend Peters stepped up to Missy's side.

"You betcha."

Each person in the room nodded. Sam smiled. There was one thing he could count on here. Lucki sure couldn't ignore the whole of Harbor Falls, North Carolina.

"All right. Here's the plan."

Chapter Fourteen

Lucki had not seen Sam for nearly a week. Deliberately. Not since the slap, which was probably the fatal blow to their relationship. She'd never slapped anyone in her life and figured it was quite possibly the ultimate humiliation.

But she was angry.

And hurt.

And it seemed as if someone else was possessing her body at that moment. She'd just hauled off and slapped the living hell out of him. Surely, he would never forgive her that.

How embarrassing!

But how embarrassing to find her love life being discussed amongst the women of her church! And that Sam had told Kathleen that there were no wedding plans—that they were just intimate friends, well, it was just more than she could take.

She was trying very hard not to be miserable.

Pinky was doing her darnedest to keep her spirits up.

Rick was even staying off her case lately, sensing, she guessed, that she needed space.

And Matt, well, Matt was just as sweet as Pinky. They even

took her to dinner one evening when she was procrastinating about going home. She was dreading pulling into her driveway, expecting that Sam might be there waiting for her. She didn't want to talk to him.

Ever.

Maybe once her parents got back home, she'd think about moving out. Find herself an apartment downtown, maybe. Something closer to work. She'd talked about it for years but just hadn't done it. Maybe now was the time.

Luckily, she'd had excuse after excuse to work late this week. She hadn't met Sam coming or going, morning or night. Things had been quiet at his house with J.J. off to camp with Spud. And with the council meeting coming up on Thursday, and all the work associated with that, she'd had little time to devote to thinking about Sam, anyway.

And, she'd even skipped church last Sunday. First time in years.

Funny, though. He'd not called.

So, she'd had virtually no contact with Sam.

Or anyone in Harbor Falls, for that matter.

It was a little unnerving. She'd been prepared for the onslaught.

Sam had been so damned persistent for so long. And now. Nothing.

So finally, she'd just decided that Sam had called it quits. It was just like before, when he'd slipped that alternate prom date in on her, and then he'd turned tail and run back to school. Now, he was just flat-out avoiding her.

Oh, well, all the better.

Now, she could just get back to her humiliating little life and suffer the collective pooh-poohs from the whole of Harbor Falls.

Thank goodness, she thought as she stared out the door of her cubicle, that the council meeting was tonight, and *that* would soon be behind her. At least then she'd have one less worry on her mind. If granted funding tonight from the city council, the county would surely follow suit next week.

At least she still had her kids. Right now, they were what kept her going.

ON SATURDAY, LUCKI DECIDED SHE SHOULD probably venture out for groceries. There was practically nothing to eat in the house. She was feeling a mite better. The council had approved her funding request Thursday evening, Rick was elated, and she was sure things would go well for them the next Tuesday at the county meeting.

That had made her week.

She had to concentrate on the good things.

She was thinking about that when she entered the automatic doors of Ralph's Grocery that Saturday morning. Maybe that's why she had a smile on her face, she wasn't sure. She'd been thinking about her kids. She was so proud of them that night at the meeting; they had handled themselves so well.

Perhaps that was why she was taken aback when Eloise Hunter approached her in the produce aisle.

"Sam back from Memphis, Lucki? I see a smile on that face."

She stopped for a second to assess Eloise's words. Sam was in Memphis? Suddenly, Eloise clamped her mouth tightly shut, as if she'd said something she shouldn't have.

"Excuse me, Eloise?"

Eloise shook her head. "Oh, nothing, Lucki. Just thinking out loud. It was nothing."

But Lucki knew it was something.

"Sam is in Memphis? I didn't know."

"Oh, I'm sure you didn't, honey." Eloise was ready to burst. She looked like the cat that had swallowed the canary.

"Spill it, Eloise. I know you want to say something."

Eloise rocked her head and clamped her lips tightly, then took off for the bread aisle. Lucki watched her skirts swish from behind as she vamoosed.

"That's odd." *Sam is in Memphis?*

She picked out a few fruits and vegetables and then followed Eloise's path at a more leisurely pace. She stopped to peruse the array of donuts. She needed some for her truck.

Her standard breakfast.

Gee, if she only had someone to fix her waffles every morning.

"So, shopping for one or two?"

Lucki jerked her head up and looked sharply to her right. Lamar Thompson stood staring at the Hostess Twinkies. "What did you say, Lamar?"

He slowly turned his head toward her. Lamar never got in a hurry. "Oh, nothing, Lucki. Nothing."

Frustrated, Lucki stared at the man, who was now turning over in his hands the box of Twinkies. "No, you said something about shopping for one or two, didn't you, Lamar?"

He took his good time answering. "No, I said I wondered whether I should buy one or two. Of the Twinkies, you know. My grandchildren are coming to visit on Monday."

Perplexed, Lucki mentally took a step back. "Oh. That's nice. Have a great time with them, Lamar."

He nodded and casually sauntered off.

Strange. Lucki shook her head and started toward the frozen foods.

She was trying to decide whether to buy pepperoni or supreme pizza when a shadow cast over her shoulder onto the pizza boxes.

"I'd buy the supreme if I were you. You know men always like lots of meat on their pizza."

She whirled.

"What in the world are you talking about, Missy?" Had all of Harbor Falls gone insane?

"Better get the large, too. But I don't think I'd rely on frozen food much longer. You know you're going to be cooking for more than one from now on. Actually three. Men always like home cooking better. Might want to take that into consideration."

Lucki screwed up her face in disbelief. "What in the hell are you talking about?"

"Just a thought, Lucki."

Then like a flash, she was gone.

Lucki wanted to scream right there in the middle of Ralph's.

She made it through the meat counter, the cereal aisle, and then through the canned goods, but when she got to the dairy case, she rounded the corner to find Kathleen perusing the assorted cheeses.

"Lucki! My goodness. I haven't seen you all week! Are you doing okay?"

A bit cautious, Lucki gauged the conversation carefully. "Yes, Kathleen. I'm fine."

"Well, you've holed yourself up like a little chipmunk all week. No one has seen hide nor hair of you, girl!"

Lucki relaxed a bit. Maybe this was going to be a normal conversation after all. "I've been extremely busy, Kathleen. Lots of work to do at the Parks Department. You see, I'm working on this thing for the kids, a new skateboard park—"

Kathleen patted her hand. "Well, that's nice, dear. Just don't wear yourself out, you know. You have a busy week ahead of you. By the way, do you have all your shots?"

Busy week?

"Shots?"

"Your immunizations. You never know when you may need them."

Kathleen was obviously hallucinating. "Kathleen, I'm sure my immunizations are up to date."

"Well, you never know, in those foreign countries you can catch all kinds of—" She clamped a hand over her mouth. "Anyway, you've got a busy week. Rest up, dear."

"Well, yes, I've got the county council meeting on Tuesday, but after that—"

Kathleen giggled and patted her hand again. "Oh, honey, you are so downright charming sometimes. You just get your rest, you hear me? You're going to need it. Oh, and by the way, do you still have that pretty pale green silk dress you wore to Mary Beauchamp's wedding last spring?"

Lucki's brain was spinning. "Green silk dress?" Where was this leading?

"Yes, Kathleen, I do. Do you want to borrow it?" She couldn't think of any other reason Kathleen would ask; however, it was most likely the dress was three sizes too small for her.

Kathleen cackled. "Heaven's no, child! Why don't you wear it to church in the morning? That is such a pretty dress. And you looked so nice in it. Such a good color for you. Think about it, okay?"

Kathleen clucked to herself and waddled toward the snack aisle.

Lucki wondered if she'd somehow fallen into the Twilight Zone. These people were nuts!

She had to get out of here. And fast.

She threw several more items into her cart on the way to the checkout counter, carefully scanned each aisle on her way, cautiously turned every corner—she wanted no more surprises. Something was going on in Harbor Falls, and everyone had turned crazy.

Herself included.

Just as she tried to cruise by the bakery section, she heard a loud scream. She nearly topped the cupcake display.

"There she is! Get her out of here!"

Just as Lucki saw Hannah Harper and Louise Palmer attempt a little dance behind the bakery counter, Reverend Peters appeared out of nowhere and seemed to guide her most reverently toward the front of the store. As well as one could glide while being on crutches.

"Lucinda! My, it's been ages. We missed you at church last week."

Lucki glanced over her shoulder. Hannah and Louise were waving their arms and shielding her view from what looked like a very large cake.

She turned to the good Reverend. Surely, he would tell her. "Reverend Peters, what in the world is wrong with these people? I mean, everyone is saying the strangest things and doing little dances and trying to herd me in the opposite direction—like you are doing right now."

Reverend Peters feigned surprise. "Lucinda, whatever are you talking about? I was just accompanying you to the checkout. Now, about in the morning. I'm trying to decide which songs we should sing. Do you prefer "Oh Promise Me" or would you like something a little more contemporary?"

"I think something more contemporary—"

Lucki stopped dead cold in the aisle.

Oh Promise Me?

She stared at Reverend Peters. "You're just like them. You're going crazy, too. Am I the only one here who is sane?"

The Reverend chuckled. "No, my dear. On the contrary. Now, let's get you checked out and don't forget, I expect to see you bright and early in the morning." He started unloading her items onto the counter. "You missed last week altogether, and you were late the week before that. Let's be on time tomorrow, all right, Lucinda?"

Lucki just nodded. She didn't know what else to do.

SHE OVERSLEPT.

And it felt good.

But two weeks in a row? Could she miss church two weeks in a row? Reverend Peters' little speech kept bouncing around in her head.

So, she got up. Took a quick shower. Made a feeble attempt at a refined hairdo.

Then she perused her closet. The green silk seemed to pop out at her like a sore thumb. What the hell. She put it on.

She ate two powdered donuts on the way to church. She really didn't care that a sprinkling of sugar fell across her chest. But she brushed at it anyway.

There seemed to be a bit more of a crowd than usual, but she found a parking place a block away.

As she exited her truck, she thought she heard music.

Someone was singing. A bit off key, but singing, no less. It sounded like Eloise. It sounded like *Oh Promise Me.*

She shook her head. Impossible.

She let herself in the back door, made her way up the stairway, and stopped just outside the choir loft. Quickly, she donned her choir robe, firmly clasped a hymnal in her hand, and waited for the music to stop. She hoped she could slip in undetected while the congregation stood for a prayer.

She waited.

The music never stopped.

She waited some more.

Eloise was going on and on and on.

She decided to peek through the door.

She cracked it. All she could see was people. And more people. And more people. Reverend Peters sure had packed them in today.

"Lucki! Where in the world have you been?"

She jumped, and the door opened more fully. Kathleen approached her from behind.

"Just waiting for Eloise to stop singing that song so I can slip into the choir loft. What are you doing back here? You don't sing in the choir."

"No, but I've been put in charge of finding you. I've looked everywhere. Finally saw your truck down the street. Don't you realize everyone is waiting for you?"

Lucki put up her hand.

"This is ridiculous. This has to stop. Everyone has been talking in circles for days. What, is going on?"

Kathleen stepped forward and jerked down the zipper on the choir robe. "Just get that thing off and come with me. You'll find out soon enough."

Lucki stepped out of the robe. She took Kathleen's hand and let her lead her through the door to the choir loft and around the altar to the front of the church. Then Kathleen slowly slipped away.

There she stood. Center of attention. All eyes were on her. What, in the world, was happening here?

Everything around her was a blur. People were everywhere. They started whispering.

And were those her parents over there in their regular spot? And Reverend Peters, why was he strategically placed in the center of the altar area? Wearing a more formal robe than usual? And was that Pinky all decked out there, too? Just a few feet away? Smiling like a Cheshire cat? My what a pretty dress, but she'd never gone to church here before.

And J.J.? Was that a suit and tie on the kid?

What the heck was going—?

On.

Lucki's brain slammed still. She took another moment or two. She glanced around. Lamar Thompson was in better-than-his-Sunday-best, right smack dab in the center of the front pew, as always. Eloise was perched at the piano, a feathered hat upon her head and a broad smile widening across her face. Kathleen had taken a seat two rows back. Hannah and Louise were standing near the rear of the church. Missy even smiled at her from a third of the way back. Even Matt and Rick were here.

Everyone was here. Except for Sam.

A door creaked open then from the opposite side of the church. All eyes turned that way. And Lucki watched as the most handsome man in the world, all decked out in a nice black tux, stepped toward her.

Her man.

Sam.

Suddenly, it all made sense.

Suddenly, she knew exactly what was going on.

Sam stepped closer and took both her hands. He cleared his throat. The entire congregation of the United Methodist Church of Harbor Falls, North Carolina, took in a collective breath. And held it.

Before he spoke, he reached up and swiped a finger across the corner of her mouth, then lifted it to his own and licked off a bit of sugar. "Powdered donuts?" He grinned, and Lucki couldn't help but relax.

Then his face grew serious again.

He got down on one knee, and popped open a ring box, showing her the prettiest diamond engagement ring she'd ever seen. Tears stung her eyes.

"Lucinda Stevenson," he whispered. "I love you. I think I always have, and I know I always will. Finally, for once and for all, will you marry me?" His voice echoed throughout the sanctuary.

Lucki searched deep into Sam's eyes. She wanted to say yes, right then and there, but could she? Surely, he was stating his intentions right here, in front of the entire town, with intention. He had to be serious, right?

"Sam..." she whispered.

He stood up and faced her eye-to-eye. "I would love to marry you today," he said. "But I know that maybe that is too much to expect. I know women like to plan these things and make everything a big hoopla with parties and all that. So I understand if you *don't* want to get married today, Lucki, but if you could just say yes, that you'll marry me *someday*, I'll be the happiest man in the world."

She glanced around again. Every person in the church sat in anticipation of her response. Waiting for her answer. The church swelled with an expectant pause. Then she looked back into Sam's face. Perspiration ran down his temple.

Oh goodness, the poor man is so nervous.

"Sam, I..." The only thing she could do was look deep into her heart. And when she did, she realized what she'd known all along. She closed her eyes.

"I love you, Lucki." He grasped her hand. "I have always loved you," he whispered. "I can't imagine my life without you, and I don't even want to think about what that would be like. Marry me?"

Her eyes fluttered open and again, she looked at Sam and exhaled. "Yes," she whispered on that breath. "Yes, Sam, I'll marry you."

The broadest grin she had ever seen spread across Sam's face. Then his expression grew serious again. "Today, or...?"

Lucki stepped closer to him and leaned in, her lips brushing his cheek. "Yes, Sam. I'll marry you today."

In one fell swoop, he wrapped his arms around her and

lifted her off her feet. "You have no idea how happy you've made me," he whispered. He sat her down then and looked longingly into her eyes. "God, I love you, Lucki. Only you."

"I love you, too, Sam."

"Do I need to explain what happened the other day?"

Lucki glanced around her. Everyone was waiting. Her mother was dabbing at her eyes. She looked back at Sam.

"No, sweetheart. You don't have to explain now. Later will be fine."

"Good. Because we have a wedding to go to, and we don't want to be late."

"No. That, we surely don't want to do," she whispered back.

Sam fiddled with the box in his hand, and Lucki's gaze followed. With nervous fingers, Sam removed the engagement ring and placed it on the third finger of her left hand, then lifted her chin with his forefinger to kiss her sweetly and gently.

"Don't we need a license or something?"

Sam nodded. "Yes, of course." He leaned closer. "I've done the paperwork but you need to sign down at the courthouse tomorrow. We can do the legal thing then. But right now? Let's have the wedding of our hearts, right here and now, in front of friends and family. What do you say?"

Lucki narrowed her gaze and whispered, "Sam Kirk if you break my heart between now and tomorrow...."

Sam held her glare. "Sweetheart, do you think I'd risk breaking your heart in front of the entire town of Harbor Falls? That would be suicide."

Slowly, Lucki grinned. "Marry me, Sam," she murmured. "Now."

"Yes, ma'am." Taking her hand, he smiled and led her toward Reverend Peters, who performed the ceremony with lightning speed. He knew the rules, of course. The time was approaching noon.

The congregation cheered at the sultry kiss that sealed the deal, and Lucki and Sam Kirk embraced each other like there was no tomorrow.

But they now had a forever full of tomorrows, and Lucki had never felt happier about that.

"I love you, Mrs. Kirk," Sam said tenderly.

"And I love you back, Dr. Kirk." She pulled back far enough to look into his eyes. "By the way, may I ask where you've been all week?"

"Memphis," he replied. "I hired another physician for the office. Now I have more time for you and J.J. And besides, we're going on a honeymoon for the next two weeks, and I'll need someone here."

"Honeymoon?"

"Jamaica."

"Really?"

"Umhmm..." He nuzzled her closer and kissed her lips again.

"Hey you too." J.J. pulled on Sam's coat. "We better get moving."

Lucki looked at Sam, questioning. What other surprises were in store for her today? "Moving?" Were they heading for the airport now?

Sam glanced at his watch. "You know, he's right. We've gotta get going."

"To Jamaica?"

Sam smiled. "No, silly. To the reception. It's at Buddy's. If we want to beat the Baptists, then we better get going."

Lucki took Sam's hand and grinned.

Finally, everything in Harbor Falls was back to normal.

A Note from Maddie

Dear Friends,

I hope you enjoyed *The Heartbreaker*. Lucki and Sam were a fun couple to write. I remember brainstorming this book with my son while we were sitting in the stands at the ballpark watching my (then) teenage daughter play baseball. Lucki was definitely patterned after her! It's difficult for me to resist the boy-next-door trope. I hope I did it well and that you thoroughly enjoyed.

If you did, then please consider sharing this book with others. One of the best ways you can do that is to leave a review at Goodreads, or at the bookstore where you purchased the book. You can also leave reviews at my website, maddie-jamesbooks.com.

Ready for more Falls Mountain books? Scroll on to read the first chapter of *Star Crossed, Book 4*.

Star Crossed

Star Crossed–Chapter One

They say you can never go home again.

Jasmine Walker stepped out of her Audi and browsed the streets of her old hometown. Determined to focus on the positive aspects of the day, all she wanted was to take care of business, and get out of Harbor Falls and back to Atlanta before nightfall.

She sniffed at the crisp mountain air drifting into the valley town from the Blue Ridge Mountains, a hint of spruce and lingering wood smoke tickling her nostrils. The nights and mornings were a bit cool now, and even though it was approaching ten o'clock in the morning, the temperature was chilly. She pulled her jacket together and buttoned it.

The breeze played with her hair for a moment. Closing her eyes, she paused to let the essence of the town settle around her. She blinked, then moved out of the way and closed the car door. She headed for the sidewalk, turned, and scanned the town once more, glancing right and left.

Settling her gaze in the opposite direction from her destination, she searched just above the treetops, traveling the length of the street. Victorian shop fronts graced both sides,

175

with mature trees, potted plants, streetlights, and awnings, complete with small-town hustle and bustle.

Some things had changed. There were a few new stores, ones that if she'd had more time, she wouldn't mind browsing —something she never did when she'd lived there. She spotted a local gift shop across the street next to a bakery, and it looked like the library might have undergone an expansion. She'd spent a lot of time there as a kid. Much of the town was the same, however, as when she'd left fifteen years earlier.

What she was looking for wasn't on the sidewalk or at the street level though, but in the distance above the buildings and trees.

There.

Ms. Leinie's house.

Her stomach clutched as her gaze drifted up behind the courthouse to the big, white house on the hill a few blocks away—the one she had once called home. Suddenly, she had to shake herself. She'd been sad to learn of Ms. Leinie's death and had it not been for the call from Art Manchester, a local attorney, Jasmine might not have known. On the other hand, she might have belatedly found out and sent a donation and simply reflected on her relationship with the old woman back in the safe confines of her condominium.

Reflecting on the positives, of course, and not the negatives.

She strived for an optimistic life. Glass half full, and all that. It hadn't always been that way.

But the call did come, and she'd made the day trip back to Harbor Falls.

An older model pick-up truck with country music blaring whizzed by, pulling her out of her musing, and reminding her of the more-than-subtle differences between Harbor Falls and Atlanta.

Jasmine glanced at her watch. She had ten minutes until

her appointment with the attorney. Turning, she headed back up Main Street but stopped long enough to push a few coins into her parking meter before moving on. Two hours should be enough. She didn't expect to be long here in Harbor Falls. There was nothing to keep her, no one to see while she was in town. She'd severed all of those ties years ago. Two hours should be ample time to deal with the business of Ms. Leinie's estate and then head back home. She had a case that needed her attention tonight.

Her heels clicked on the sidewalk as she made her way down the street, a nagging question lingering in her head.

Why, after all this time, had Leinie Crockett decided to leave anything to her?

"So, you broke up with her?"

Jack Ackerman winced at his brother's question. Instead of immediately responding, he stared ahead through the windshield and concentrated on driving down the two-lane road on Harbor Falls Mountain. He really wasn't up to talking much about the recent events with Miss Nora Patterson.

"Jack?"

"I figured you knew."

"No. Not until this morning when Mom called."

Hell. He braked for a curve and nearly threw his brother into the door. "Mom called?"

"She heard it down at Ralph's."

"Shit." He twisted the radio button to crank up Blake Shelton, hoping to drown out the noise starting to clatter in his head. That's all he needed, for every woman of marrying age in Harbor Falls to be on his tail. How many single, thirty-four-year-old men were there out there, anyway? Not many.

And he didn't need the grocery store gossipmongers on the trail.

They traveled along for several minutes, turning at the foot of the mountain to head along Lake Road, and then into downtown Harbor Falls. They each needed to run a couple of errands and then get back out to Haven's Hill to prep for a big landscaping job at Suzie Hart's Sweet Hart Inn later in the week. Seemed she was hosting some fancy to-do with some New York bigwigs, and all that. He wouldn't let his friend down.

Finally, he glanced at Sam. "Yeah. We broke up."

Sam shrugged. "I don't get it."

"It's for the best."

"Becca never said a word."

That surprised him. Becca and Nora being best friends and all, and Becca being Sam's wife. "Guess that kills our euchre game night."

He saw Sam's nod out of the corner of his eye. Jack slowed as he approached Main Street and searched for a street parking space.

"Over there by the bank." Sam nodded that way.

"Want me to drop you off at the hardware store?"

"Naw, I'll walk."

Jack parallel parked the pickup and turned to Sam. "Guess I'll have to ditch out of that couples thing up at the lodge on Saturday too. Hope you and Becca understand. Not sure I'm up for it."

Sam's brows furled. "That woman do a number on you?"

He shook his head. "Nope. It was mutual, actually. The relationship wasn't going anywhere, and honestly, I wasn't in love with her. Not like you are in love with Becca." *I want more. Like kids. The picket fence. Normal.*

"There will be a lot of women up there at the lodge on Saturday." Sam waggled his brows.

"It's a couples thing, remember?"

"Sure, but it's a benefit for the hospital, so I don't think they'll kick you out on your ear because you don't have a date."

Jack winced. "Yeah but count me out. Not in the mood."

"Ah. That's all right." Sam opened the truck door. "I'll meet you back here in about twenty minutes. Just need a pair of long screws."

Jack chuckled and watched his brother head down the sidewalk. *You and me both, buddy.*

Jasmine, 1999

Breathless, I pushed into the kitchen, letting the back screen door slap a mite too hard behind me. "Oops! So sorry Ms. Leinie." I'd practically sprinted the whole way home from school, nearly giddy at what I knew the future held for me.

"Jasmine! Honey, what's the hurry?"

Ms. Leinie turned away from the stove and smiled. In so many ways, I hated thinking about leaving, because Ms. Leinie had really been the only woman to ever influence my life—but graduation was just three weeks away.

It's inevitable. I'm aging out of foster care and I have to think of my future.

Stepping to the refrigerator, I said, "I know you are cooking but I'm starved. Mind if I have an apple? You know I have an appetite from hell and it won't spoil my supper." I reached for the handle.

"Lord knows you have a bottomless pit for a stomach, girl. Go ahead. And don't say 'hell'."

"Sorry." Ms. Leinie liked all of us kids to keep our mouths clean. "It's from running track. I burn it all off."

"You been running this afternoon? You're all hot and sweaty." She stirred the pot and side-glanced at me.

Removing an apple from the fruit bin, I stepped to the sink to wash it off, then moved closer to the stove and glanced into the pot. "Oh, vegetable soup. Homemade. I love you, Ms. Leinie." I threw my arms around her next and kissed her cheek.

Her skin was paper-thin and reminded me of tissue paper. I wasn't sure how old Ms. Leinie was, but I guessed her to be in her late sixties. She was a practical woman and dressed simply, with her hair pulled back. There were days I wondered how long it was, because most times I saw it in a clip and off her face. It was white-gray, but I could see wisps of dark curls at the nape of her neck. There were times I would sit and study her while she didn't know I was looking. I imagined in her younger years, she was a striking woman.

I often wondered what my mother would have looked like as an older woman.

"No, not running today. Just hurrying to get home and it's heating up out there for May. But I have some exciting news! You have to promise me you won't tell anyone. It's like a pinky-swear thing."

Ms. Leinie looked at me and grinned. "Well now, I haven't had to pinky-swear on anything in a long time. What's up, Jasmine? I bet you got that music award."

"No. No." I grinned. "Well, maybe. They won't announce those until graduation night. I'm still in the running for it and the cash could really help with my college expenses." I paused and watched as she nodded in agreement but couldn't contain my excitement any longer. The words bubbled out. "Jack asked me to marry him. We're getting married."

Her face fell. And something icky landed in the pit of my stomach.

She reached for my hand. "Jasmine, honey, come sit down

and let's talk about this." She tugged at my hand, but I couldn't move. Her tone, her words...none if it was good. My excitement was abruptly squashed.

After a moment, I found my feet, drifted toward the table, and sat.

She looked me in the eyes and patted my hand. "You know the Ackermans are never going to allow this marriage. Right?"

She'd warned me before about the Ackermans. I'd met both of Jack's parents and his older brother Sam. Most of the time I just saw them from afar at the ball games and in town. They were always nice but distant. I knew why. I tried not to let it bother me.

Jack had been my boyfriend since football season. I played flute in the band, and he, of course, was on the team. The band went to all of the away games, and before I knew it, we were catching each other's gazes, and it didn't take long for us to become a couple. Jack loved me for who I am, no matter what. We were head-over-heels in love, as they say. "Well, that's why we're waiting until graduation is finished to really make any plans. They don't know yet, and Jack isn't going to tell them right away. We'll get married this summer and then move to Asheville and go to school. We'll get jobs and support ourselves. We'll be fine."

The look on her face puzzled me. Then she said, "Jasmine, think about this. Because you are in foster care, the state will take care of your college expenses, and all of that. But if you get married, all of that stops. How will you support yourself and pay for college at the same time? You don't want to discount all of that. Why don't you and Jack just wait?"

I'd already thought about all of that. "It's okay. I have it all worked out. I don't want to rely on the state if I don't have to. I want to be self-sufficient. Besides, there are work study programs that I've already applied to and I'm eligible for, and I will get the Social Security income from my mom, plus I get a little money because of Dad...."

Ms. Leinie interrupted. "Jasmine, I understand all of that. It's just—"

I smiled and tried to look upbeat. "It will be fine! Really!"

But she wasn't buying it. "Honey, I fear you are setting yourself up for a whole world of hurt. I don't want your sweet little heart to get broken. I swear, sometimes you can be so gullible. The Ackermans are never going to accept this."

Gullible?

I felt a little prickly inside, defensive, and unsure why I felt the need to state my case. Ms. Leinie wasn't the enemy, and I knew fully well how Jack's parents felt. I stood up. "It doesn't matter. Jack and I love each other, and—"

"You don't have to leave here, Jasmine," she interrupted. "Don't get married because you think you don't have a home. You can stay here until you get on your feet. You're still so young."

"Ms. Leinie. It's not that. I love Jack."

She stood then, too, and took both of my hands in hers. She shook them gently. "Jasmine, you listen to me. I have to be honest. You've been with me for so long, and I feel like your mama in so many ways. I'm going to talk to you like a mama would. Let Jack go off to college, you too, and then later, down the road, if you feel the same about each other, think about getting married then. Live some life first. Don't tie yourself down."

I eyed her, watching the concern grow on her face. "Being young is not what you're concerned about, is it, Ms. Leinie? You know Jack's parents don't like me. You know they think I'm not good enough for Jack, considering my background. But Jack loves me. We love each other. That's all that matters, right?"

Her eyes welled up with tears. She pulled me closer and

hugged me. I remember that hug well because it was the last one she ever gave me. It was warm and firm, but laced with a strange sense of desperation and apprehension.

She pulled back. "Honey, I love your heart, but not everyone has the giving and kind heart that you do. If you marry Jack, I fear your happy heart will turn. The Ackermans won't—"

"Just say it, Ms. Leinie. Just say what's on your mind."

Her lips clamped shut. I stared at her until she finally did say it.

"Okay. Jasmine, this is a small town. You know this. And even though it's almost the 21st century, it's still the conservative south. There are a lot of people who are not so liberal. The Ackermans are like that. And well..." She paused and took a deep breath. I knew where this was going. I didn't breathe at all for many seconds. "Well," she continued, "they are not going to stand by and let their youngest boy run off and get married to...you."

"To me."

She nodded slowly, a pained expression on her face. "To a little mixed girl."

A little mixed girl.

My heart turned right then, on the spot. I broke the grasp with Ms. Leinie's hands and slowly backed away, our gazes connected. I knew she didn't mean to sound so harsh, but in my naïve little heart, that's how I took it.

"You mean a half-breed, Black girl don't you?" Because she'd always be half-Black, but never half-white.

She took a step forward. "Jasmine."

I backed off.

"Fine," I said, right before I left the kitchen, "then I'll just take my poor half-white trash self out of this town and by God, I will not look back. Thank you for everything, Ms. Leinie."

Then I turned and raced for the stairs, knowing I was placing the blame where it shouldn't be placed, saying things that made no sense. I heard her calling after me, but the white noise in my head wouldn't let her words in.

Learn more about *Star Crossed* on my website, or purchase at your favorite bookstore.

More Harbor Falls Books

Cozy up at the inn where the heart of the Blue Ridge beats strongest...

Welcome to Sweet Hart Inn, a charming bed and breakfast nestled along the peaceful shores of Falls Lake, at the foot of Falls Mountain. At the center of it all is chef and innkeeper Suzie Hart, whose kitchen is always warm, and whose heart is always open. Together with her husband Brad, Suzie serves up matchmaking advice and comfort food, along with second chances, and a generous helping of happily ever after.

The Sweet Hart Inn Books

All of My Heart
Take My Heart
Match My Heart
Tame My Heart
The Dating Game
Miss Matched Hearts
The Husband List
Chase My Heart
No Sweeter Match
One More Kiss

The Falls Mountain Books

Welcome to Falls Mountain, and the quaint town of Harbor Falls.

Tucked deep into the Blue Ridge Mountains, bricked streets, lakeside views, and charming local shops set the scene for small town romance.

In this standalone-but-interconnected series, you'll meet bakers, bookstore owners, chocolatiers, school teachers, and more—all trying to run their businesses, chase their dreams, and keep their hearts in check. But in Harbor Falls, love has a habit of showing up unannounced...

From second chances to secret babies to grumpy-sunshine pairings, each book brings a satisfying happily-ever-after and a cast of characters you'll want to visit again and again.

Falls Mountain Romance is a companion series to the Sweet Hart Inn Romance books by Maddie James.

Dance into My Heart
The Christmas Nanny
The Heartbreaker

Star Crossed
Not This Christmas
Convince My Heart

I hope you'll check out these books, and my other series, on my website at:
www.maddiejamesbooks.com

About Maddie James

Romance with a pulse—small towns, big love, and a dash of drama.

Maddie James writes small-town romance with heart, heat, and the occasional haunting. Her stories range from sweet to spicy, suspenseful to supernatural—happily-ever-afters guaranteed! From stand-alone love stories to binge-worthy series, Maddie delivers love next door, some cowboy kisses, an occasional hint of danger, and just enough drama to keep things interesting.

Get all the drama delivered to your inbox when you sign-on to Maddie's VIP reader list!

Free books, sneak peaks, bonus content, giveaways, and more...

Learn more: maddiejamesbooks.com/pages/newsletter